CRACKHEAD

ALSO BY LISA LENNOX

Crackhead II

Played

CRACKHEAD

A Novel

LISA LENNOX

ATRIA PAPERBACK
New York • London • Toronto • Sydney • New Delhi

ATRIA PAPERBACK
A Division of Simon & Schuster, Inc.
1230 Avenue of the Americas
New York, NY 10020

This book is a work of fiction. Names, characters, places, and incidents either are products of the author's imagination or are used fictitiously. Any resemblance to actual events or locales or persons, living or dead, is entirely coincidental.

Originally published in 2004 by Triple Crown Publications.

Published by arrangement with Triple Crown Publications.

First Atria Paperback edition March 2012

ATRIA PAPERBACK and colophon are trademarks of Simon & Schuster, Inc.

For information about special discounts for bulk purchases, please contact Simon & Schuster Special Sales at 1-866-506-1949 or business@simonandschuster.com.

The Simon & Schuster Speakers Bureau can bring authors to your live event. For more information or to book an event, contact the Simon & Schuster Speakers Bureau at 1-866-248-3049 or visit our website at www.simonspeakers.com.

Manufactured in the United States of America

10 9 8 7 6 5 4 3 2

Library of Congress Cataloging-in-Publication Data
Lennox, Lisa.
Crackhead : a novel / Lisa Lennox. — 1st Atria Books trade paperback ed.
p. cm.
1. Drug addicts—Fiction. 2. Young women—Fiction. 3. African American women—Fiction. 4. Bronx (New York, NY)—Fiction. 5. Urban fiction. I. Title.
PS3612.E5496C7 2012
813'.6—dc23 2011035095

ISBN: 978-1-4516-6173-6
ISBN: 978-1-4516-6174-3 (ebook)

This book goes out to all those addicted to crack cocaine—
with God all things are possible.

FOREWORD

STUDIES SHOW THAT animals addicted to cocaine preferred the drug to food even when it meant possible starvation, and many users of its second cousin, crack, report being hooked after only the first use. This horrible addiction is three-fold: psychological, physical, and emotional.

The College of Communication, Boston University, September 1989

CRACKHEAD

INTRODUCTION

Roll Call

THE LAST FEW students stumbled into Mr. Giencanna's Introduction to Philosophy class like zombies. It was only 9:30 a.m.—still too goddamn early in the morning to be trying to philosophize over some shit. No one felt like being there. Unfortunately, taking this class, not to mention dealing with Mr. Giencanna, was a necessary evil. Mr. Giencanna was one of those teachers that taught a little bit of everything, and no matter what, all students would cross his path sooner or later.

Standing at the front of the room, staring mercilessly at the students, Mr. Giencanna stood in his usual hard-ass stance. He had been a counselor at a boy's home in New York City before becoming a teacher. The children there were violent and hardened, and the staff treated them as such. Now, Mr. Giencanna displayed that same attitude with his current students.

Observing the angry mob of young adults, who seemed more pissed off about learning than being grateful for it, Mr. Giencanna shook his head. "Look at you all," he said with disgust.

"Not one enthusiastic face in here eager to feed his or her mind. If you don't feed your mind, then how are you going to feed your belly when it comes time to survive on your own?" The room was filled with blank faces, and there was no response. "Mark my words," he continued, "without knowledge you're all bound for the welfare line or the penitentiary." Nobody was trying to hear him, and he proceeded with the daily roll call.

"Mr. Jason Abbott?" Mr. Giencanna called out, fixing his glasses on his hawklike nose.

"Here," a young man in the rear spoke up.

"Casey Bernard?"

"Right here," said another male's voice.

"Miss Natalie Farmer?"

This time there was no reply.

"Natalie Farmer?" he repeated.

A young man wearing a blue and gray varsity jacket nudged Natalie, who was at her desk, dozing off.

"What?" she said sleepily, and with an attitude.

He nodded toward their instructor. "Roll call. That's what," he replied.

"I'm here, Mr. Giencanna, sir," Natalie said, wiping around her mouth.

"Stay with us, please, Miss Farmer," said Mr. Giencanna. Although he phrased it like a request, Natalie knew by his stern tone and the piercing look in his eyes that it was, without a doubt, an order.

Mr. Giencanna cleared his throat and continued. "Miss Julacia Johnson?"

Once again there was no reply. The classroom was silent as everyone looked around to see if there was another nodding student somewhere. Everyone appeared to be wide awake.

"Perhaps we have another sleeping beauty amongst us," Mr. Giencanna said sarcastically. "Is there a Miss Julacia Johnson present?"

Still there was no reply.

"Julacia Johnson?" he repeated, very much irritated this time. The silence remained.

The welfare line or the penitentiary, he thought as he prepared to call the next name.

CHAPTER 1

Diamond Girl

"SO, TALK TO me, Laci. We have a lot to discuss," Laci's mother, Margaret, said as she sat down Indian-style on the edge of Laci's bed. She looked more like one of Laci's peers than she did her mother.

"What do you mean 'a lot'?" Laci said as she fumbled through the endless name-brand clothes in her oversized walk-in closet—Gucci, Fendi, Troop, Liz Claiborne, Guess. She was in the process of throwing out old clothes that she hadn't worn in a while or that were worn out. She had to make room for the new ones she planned on purchasing during their annual mother-daughter shopping spree. Summer and college were right around the corner, and she would need a new wardrobe to set things off.

"Just what I said—a lot," Margaret said, smiling. "I want to know everything."

"Everything, like what?" Laci asked, intentionally stalling.

"Like whether you've decided where you want to go for the graduation trip I'm sending you on. Like, do you have a boyfriend who might want to go on the trip with you?" Margaret leaned in, looking for some kind of response in her daughter's face.

"I knew you were fishing for something," Laci said as she flung a handful of clothes from her closet onto the floor.

"Well, you're only the most beautiful seventeen-year-old girl in the world," her mother said proudly. "And I'm not just saying that because I was a model and you are my daughter."

Julacia, or Laci, as she was called, was indeed very attractive. She was small in stature and had a face like a porcelain doll. Her long, black, shiny Shirley Temple–like curls cascaded across the left side of her forehead, tickling her perfectly arched eyebrow. Her moody brown eyes complimented her light butterscotch skin tone. She was often mistaken for being Puerto Rican. In 1989, there weren't exactly a whole bunch of biracial kids walking around. Laci could have fit right in with Pebbles or Mariah Carey, with her light skin with "good" hair. At 5′4″, Laci was thick and curvy in all the right places. She was tight-to-def with junk in the trunk, a slim waist, and nice B-cup breasts. Though never one to be conceited, Laci knew she had a bangin' body and a funky fresh style to match. She would look good even if she were dressed in rags.

"Mom . . ." Laci said wearily.

"Tell me, tell me, tell me," her mother asked anxiously, bouncing on the bed like a giddy teenager. "What's his name? What does he look like?"

"What are you talking about?" Laci said, sucking her teeth. "There is no *he.* And you know you'd be the first to know if there was."

"So you say," Margaret replied, giving Laci a doubtful look.

"Mom, I'm not seeing anybody." Laci had sadness in her eyes.

"Come on, baby," Margaret said with a wink. "I'm not only

your mother, but your friend, too. All we have is each other. I love being a part of your life. In a way, I live through you. You make me feel like *I'm* seventeen again. So, get to talkin', honey. Is he tall, short, thin, buff, or what?"

"Mom," Laci whined, stepping out of the closet with an old sundress in her hand. "I don't have a boyfriend." She threw the dress in the pile she had started on the floor, then walked over to her bed and crawled to the middle of it.

"Okay, if you say you're not seeing anybody, then I'll have to believe you." Margaret grabbed Laci's old Cabbage Patch doll that was lying on the bed. "So where are you going on your vacation? Have you thought of someplace nice?"

"I was thinking of Puerto Rico," Laci said excitedly.

"Ooh, that sounds nice. So should I go ahead and book a ticket for you . . . and your boyfriend?" Margaret started kissing the doll. Laci laughed and playfully threw a pillow at her. "Oh, boy, you shouldn't have done that. You don't want to tell me who your boyfriend is, huh? Then take that!" She pounded Laci repeatedly with a pillow and began to laugh hysterically.

"Mom, please stop," Laci pleaded. "You're messing up my hair!"

"If you didn't have a boyfriend, then you wouldn't care how your hair looked. Now, what's his name?" Margaret asked out of breath, getting in another hit.

"Wait, wait," Laci said, reaching for her ringing Mickey Mouse phone on the nightstand next to the bed. "Hello?" she said, catching her breath.

"Hey, Laci?" the voice on the other end said.

"Yes, this is she," Laci replied, not recognizing the voice. "Who is this?"

"Girl, its Monique," said the smiling voice. "What you doin'?"

"Laci," her mother called from behind her, "You want to catch a movie or go to dinner tonight? You know . . . celebrate your upcoming graduation, going off to Boston?"

"Hold on, Monique," Laci said, covering the phone. "What'd you say, Mom?"

"I said do you wanna go out and celebrate tonight? With graduation right around the corner and you going off to college, I figured that was cause enough for us to get out of this house and go do something."

"Okay, Mom. After I get off the phone, we'll see." Laci then directed her attention back to the phone. "Monique . . . you still there?" Laci's mother hit her again with a pillow, which landed on the bed. Laci tried to hurry up and grab the pillow to get the last hit, but her mother was too quick and ran out of the room.

"Yeah, I'm here," Monique answered.

"Okay, girl," Laci said, chuckling and breathing hard.

"Why you breathing so hard?"

"Fooling around with my crazy mother. We were having a pillow fight," Laci giggled. "She wants to take me out tonight."

As usual, Monique tried to twist Laci's words around. "Why you try'na throw shit up in my face?" she snapped.

Laci should have seen it coming. Of all the girls in Tonette's crew (which included Shaunna, Crystal, Monique, and of course Tonette), Monique seemed to be the most envious of Laci's relationship with her mother.

Monique had been living with her grandmother for the last few years. Her mother died when she was just a freshman in high school. Not an addict herself, Monique's mother had made the all-too-common mistake of sleeping with a dope fiend, who was infected with some mysterious new virus called HIV.

"What are you talking about?" Laci asked, getting sick of Monique's attitude.

"*What are you talking about?*" Monique replied, mimicking Laci's proper English. "You sound like a white girl."

"Look," Laci huffed, "was there a reason for this call, or did you just feel like starting another argument?"

"Never mind," Monique said, sucking her teeth. "You ain't gon' wanna go. Forget it. I didn't mean to interrupt your pillow fight. Go hang out with your *mommy.* I need to call the rest of the crew to make sure they're wit' it. Peace out."

Laci was confused. Her face revealed the frustration she endured on a daily basis as a result of interacting with her homegirls. It was safe to say that she was the prima donna of the pack. She definitely had the most going for her; sweet and laid back, Laci was the complete opposite of her loud, foul-mouthed friends from the South Bronx. Born with a silver spoon in her mouth, Laci was living the lifestyle of the rich and famous compared to her girls. Her mother was white and a former model featured in such magazines as *Sports Illustrated, Cosmopolitan,* and *Glamour.* Her dad, Jay Johnson, was black and a corporate lawyer. As the only child, Laci got whatever she wanted, even if she didn't ask for it. After her father died of a massive heart attack, mother and daughter moved back to Riverdale, one of New York City's wealthier neighborhoods, also located in the Bronx. Although Laci and her girls lived in the same borough, they lived worlds apart.

It probably would have been in her best interest to not associate with a group of around-the-way girls. Being connected with one of the Bronx's most well-known female crews, it was also probably in her best interest to be seen and not heard. No matter what came out of Laci's mouth, it was always viewed as her being bougie, uppity, a snob. Wanting so badly to be a part of something blinded her to the point where she couldn't see that not everybody was down for her. Some of those girls wanted to be her, and it was only a matter of time before jealousy would rear its ugly head.

Laci was so taken aback by Monique's negative attitude that she didn't even notice her mother come back into the bedroom. "Laci, what's the matter?" Margaret asked, noticing the sudden change in her disposition.

"Uh, nothing," Laci lied.

"Laci . . ." Her mother had that *I know you're lying* tone in her voice.

Laci sighed. "It's just that the girls are always so confrontational with me. Everything I say is bad. Like when they ask me questions, it's almost like they do it just to argue with me," she said in frustration.

"I don't understand," her mother said, leaning in the doorway with her arms folded. "Give me an example of what you're talking about."

"Like us having money, or you and I being so close." Laci sighed again, falling back on the bed.

"What about us?" Margaret asked, confused.

"When I talk about you and me going shopping, they get all uptight. They don't have any money. I'm tired of being sorry for not being poor."

"Really?" Margaret asked, concerned. She walked over to the bed and sat down next to Laci. "I didn't know this about your new friends."

Laci nodded. "And I don't care about that, Mom. I just want to hang with them, you know? When's the last time you've known me to have a group of friends?" Margaret remained silent. "Exactly." Laci sighed again.

"And why is it that you want to hang out with them? I'm sure there are plenty of nice kids at your school."

Laci thought for a moment. "Because . . . I don't know. The kids I go to school with are really stuck up, plus, they're racist. I just like hanging out with more down-to-earth people I can relate and talk to. I love talking to you, but I need girls my age to kick it with."

"I know you're more intelligent than that," Margaret said, hating the fact that her daughter was falling into the trap of wanting to be associated with the in-crowd. "I've never picked your friends for you, but the writing is on the wall. If a group or a person isn't good for you, then you don't need to be around them. Are you telling me that you don't care how they treat you—that you're willing to accept whatever to be a part of their little crew?"

Laci let out a deep sigh. "Mom, please don't lecture me—not today."

"Okay . . . okay." Margaret threw her hands up in surrender as she got up from the bed and walked over to the door. "You're old enough to handle yourself. I'm not gonna tell you what to do, but I will tell you to be careful. You're my daughter and I love you. You know I'm here for you if you need me, Julacia."

"Yeah, I know," Laci said, turning over onto her stomach and resting her chin on her hands.

"I'll always be here for you . . . no matter what."

MARGARET TRIED TO get Laci out of the house at least once a week to go shopping, to the movies, or for a special dinner of her choice at the Russian Tea Room, Tavern on the Green, or Windows on the World at the World Trade Center. She thought it was just what her seventeen-year-old daughter needed after such a traumatic year. Laci's father had passed away eight months prior. Then, the family was living in Philadelphia, where Jay Johnson was a successful and well-known corporate attorney, one of the few in town who were black. Depressed and longing to return to where she'd grown up, Margaret packed up Laci and moved back to New York.

This particular night, the two of them had decided to go see *Beaches.* Laci was standing in line at the cineplex for popcorn, while her mother was in the bathroom, when she noticed that the girl in front of her had forgotten her change. Laci scooped up the $39.25 and chased behind the girl, who was juggling a large tub of popcorn and two sodas. The girl was both shocked and impressed. Most people, rich or poor, would have taken that money and spent it at the concession stand or pocketed it. The girl had never met anyone that honest.

"You ain't originally from here, are you?" she asked Laci.

"No," Laci blushed. "I just moved here six months ago."

"Where do you live?"

"Riverdale."

"Oh, okay." *Damn, this bitch must be paid,* the girl thought. "My name is Tonette."

"Hi Tonette, I'm Julacia."

"Jew—what?" Tonette had the only screw face.

"Jul—never mind, you can call me Laci."

"So, Laci, you here with a crew?"

"No, no crew." Laci looked down and noticed the letters *SBB.* on Tonette's satin baseball jacket. "I just go to school and hang out with my mom. She's in the bathroom. You can meet her if you like; she'll be out in a minute. Are you?"

"Am I what?"

"Are you with a crew?"

"Hell, yeah. I'm the leader of the infamous South Bronx Bitches."

"Oh." Laci had never heard a girl cuss like that, and in public, too.

Tonette nodded her head politely and thought for a minute. *She definitely don't have nothing in common with me and my crew, but I know she got cheddar.* "Say, Laci . . . check it, what school you go to?"

"Riverdale Country Day School."

Hell yeah, this bitch is rich. Tonette smiled. "Well, let's exchange numbers. Maybe we can hang out sometime. My girls and me is watching *I'm Gonna Git You Sucka.* You should hurry up, it started already."

"Oh, me and my mom are here to see *Beaches.*"

Tonette had to laugh to herself. "I see. Well, we're trying to get into something after the movie. You're free to join us. As a matter of fact you got a drink coming on me. What do you drink?"

"Coke or Pepsi," Laci said, shrugging her shoulders. "It doesn't matter to me."

This time, Tonette couldn't hold in her laugh. She and her homegirls had been drinking since the sixth grade. Nonetheless, Tonette still extended her invitation. "Well, we gon' be right outside when the movie's out. You got a pen? Take my number down."

"Great. After my mother meets you I'm sure she won't mind me hanging out with you and your crew for a while."

Fat chance, Tonette thought. "No doubt." With that she smiled, said good-bye, and returned to Crystal, Shaunna, and

Monique, who'd sent her to get some food because they'd just finished smoking some herb and had a bad case of the munchies.

The next day, Laci called Tonette, who then invited her to a high school basketball game. Ever since then, Laci had been spending a good amount of time chillin' with her new homegirls in the South Bronx.

CHAPTER 2

Follow the Leader

YO, NETTE, THIS is Crystal."

"What's good?" Tonette asked.

"Nothing much, I just hung up with Monique."

"Yeah, I talked to her about an hour ago. I'm sitting here getting dressed now, fixin' to head your way. What time everybody else supposed to be shootin' through?"

"In a bit," Crystal said. "Everybody but Laci, anyway. Monique called her up, but she be always letting her personal feelings get in the way of business."

"What *business*?" Tonette said as she held the phone between her ear and shoulder, slipping on her bright red high-top Reebok Classics.

"Hey, is Dame around?" Crystal whispered.

"Yeah, he's in the shower," Tonette said.

"Perfect!" Crystal said enthusiastically.

"Damn, girl, what's up with you?" She knew her girl was up to something. Since Tonette had moved in with Dame over a year ago, Crystal never asked about him when she called. Tonette was the nucleus, the leader of the crew. Everyone met through her; each of them had been her friend first. It was rare that they came up with an idea without her.

Tonette had a small build and a toffee-colored complexion. When she wanted to, she could be a straight-up bitch, the devil's livest advocate, but she also had the soft, winning smile of an angel. Her bright white teeth sparkled, and they rivaled her light-gray eyes. She looked a little like Vanessa Williams, wearing a part down the middle of her relaxed, shoulder-length hair. Without a doubt, Tonette was rough around the edges. Although she was a little tomboyish, her femininity shined through. She had her beautiful smile to thank for that. She always wore Jordache jeans and Reebok sneakers with either a colorful tank top in the summer or an oversized sweatshirt in the winter. Then there was the jewelry—name-plate herringbone chains, door knockers, and gold bangles.

"Well, while Monique and I were talking, something came to mind." Crystal started smirking and rubbing her hands together like some mad scientist. "Let me run it by you real quick. I think I'm going to need you to solicit Dame's help—unknowingly, of course."

After ending her call with Crystal and hearing exactly what she had in mind, Tonette sat on the bed for a moment and thought about how to execute the plan. Dame was still in the shower. He was worse than some women with his long-ass showers, and this was the perfect time for her to do what she needed to do without him knowing. Tonette was a bad bitch, but Dame was a beast. She knew that if he caught her snooping through his shit he'd beat her ass like she was some nigga.

Tonette wasn't totally comfortable with Crystal's plan, but she, too, at times felt that the only reason Laci hung around them was to make herself feel important, and that she was secretly sitting back laughing at them. Well, it was about time somebody had a laugh at her expense.

After tiptoeing over to the bathroom, she put her ear up against the door. She could hear the shower still running, and Dame was singing the hook to one of the songs from the movie *Colors*.

"Dame!" Tonette called out.

"What?" he grumbled. "You know I'm in the shower."

"I was just going to ask you if you wanted me to roll a herb," she lied, "but never mind."

Dame didn't trust anyone—especially a bitch. His antennas were always going up, alerting him to something shady. There was something in Tonette's voice that made him cut his shower short.

Tonette didn't know where Dame kept his stash because he was always moving it. She searched several different spots before he got out of the shower. She looked through his 8 Ball jacket pockets, under the mattress, and in his Adidas shoe boxes—nothing. She went through his sock drawer and VHS rack and still couldn't find it. Starting to sweat and growing more nervous, she took a seat on his workout bench and noticed something different with the television. The back of it was cracked open. Listening for Dame, she tried the back of the set, and sure enough, it popped off. *Jackpot!* she thought. Removing the ziplock bag, she took two vials from it. Then she heard the shower shut off. Shaken, she returned the baggie to its place and sealed the television back up. Before he'd stepped completely out of the bathroom, Tonette dashed for the bed, tripped over one of Dame's dumbbells, and fell to the floor. Acting like she was slingin' on the corner and the po-po had just rolled up on her, Tonette placed the capsules in her mouth, one on each side of her cheek. That was a trick she'd learned from her days working for Dame on the block.

"What the fuck you doin'?" Dame asked as he strode into the room, nude and wet. Dame was a short man, built like a stone gargoyle. He had thick arms and legs and a barrel-shaped chest. His beady eyes bore into Tonette, waiting for an answer.

"Oh, you scared me," she gasped. "I didn't hear you get out of the shower." Dame just stood there, piercing her with his eyes, waiting on a response. "I was trying to see if I left my purple thong over here. Maybe it fell under the bed. You seen it? Maybe it's at the other apartment."

Dame was really suspicious now. Tonette knew damn well that the other apartment was off-limits to her. That was where he kept his shit, his quantity, his real weight. She had been there a time or two, when he had to stop and take care of some business and she just happened to be rolling with him. But that was the last place any of her shit would be.

"I've looked everywhere and can't find it," Tonette continued. "I can't wear my purple bra without the matching thong. You sure you ain't seen it?"

Dame responded by grabbing Tonette from off the floor and running his hands all over her body, feeling for something that she wasn't supposed to have. When he came up empty, he kissed her and flicked his tongue throughout her mouth. Tonette didn't expect him to go that far, but she was ready for it nonetheless. Her tongue skills were superior, and she led the oral dance, preventing Dame from feeling the capsules.

Tonette didn't get away that easily, though. All of the touching and tonguing made Dame horny. He began to rub on Tonette, letting her know he wanted sex and she would have to give it to him. Capsules in her mouth or not, he had to get broke off. She bent over the bed and let Dame handle his business.

GRUDGINGLY, MONIQUE CALLED Laci again. This time, Laci's mother answered the phone and went into her room, telling her to take the call.

"Laci?" Monique asked timidly.

"Yeah, Monique?"

Laci's mother stood in the doorway. Just in case it was one of those ghetto bitches trying to fuck with her daughter again, she was going to snatch the phone and give them a piece of her mind.

"Yeah." Monique hesitated. "It's me. Listen, about earlier . . . I'm sorry. I had some shit on my mind and I didn't mean to take it out on you."

A smile came across Laci's face. "Don't worry about it. We all have our days," she said, glad for the apology.

"Yeah. Listen, Laci. The reason I called you earlier was to tell you that we're gonna get together at Crystal's house in a few. We wanted you to come through. You know, we just gonna do a girl's-night thing."

Laci looked down at her Movado watch with a single diamond in the face, a Sweet Sixteen present from her father. Engraved with the words "It's time to let you fly," it was a symbol of Laci approaching adulthood. It was the most expensive gift her father had ever gotten her, and she treasured it.

"I don't know," Laci sighed. She wanted to say that she and her mother were about to go out, but she didn't want to hit another one of Monique's nerves. "Well, what time?"

“We all just getting dressed and heading over to Crystal’s,” Monique said.

Laci looked at her mother, who was still standing in the doorway. “Okay,” she said hesitantly. “I’ll be there.”

Her mother knew what was up by the look on Laci’s face. She didn’t beef. She just walked over to Laci, kissed her forehead, and left. Margaret knew she had to sit back and try not to run her daughter’s life. She knew Laci would make mistakes and needed to make them in order to grow. She only hoped that Laci wouldn’t go over the deep end.

CHAPTER 3

God Bless the Child

WAYNE HAD SEEN his mother, Gloria, bring home replacement fathers, one after another. By the time he was seventeen, fifteen of his years had been spent watching them come and go. Early on, he paid no mind to their comings and goings, but as his teenage years rolled around, he began to recognize and accept what his mother's intentions were for the men in her life.

Strapped for cash, Wayne's mother did the best she could to support herself and her son with no help from friends or family. All she had was Uncle Sam's handout to work with. Women in her position were known, and sometimes expected, to swallow their pride and go from man to man until they found one who was willing to take on some of their burdens. Men, on the other hand, knew that a single mother was an easy target. She'd put up with a man's mess if she felt that it would keep him around, which in the end it usually didn't.

The men Gloria brought around found it difficult to be the man of the house, especially since it was clear that they didn't want the responsibility or plan on staying that long. In Gloria's case, as in most cases, the cat would hang around until the sex got stale, and then move on to the next victim. Sometimes things would even get violent.

A couple of years ago, when Wayne was fifteen, his mother had brought a man named Buck home. The man of the hour, Buck stood 6′1″, was sloppy and overweight, and had a lazy left eye. The only reason he was able to get at Gloria in the first place was because his money put meat in the freezer. Gloria was numb to the physical appearance of men if they proved useful to her. It didn't matter what they looked like or how much they weighed. The only thing Gloria saw was dollar signs, and as far as she was concerned, all money looked alike and spent the same—quick and easy. Those same words also could have been used to describe her. She was quick to find a man and easy enough for him to have his way with her. Buck was no exception.

Wayne was wise beyond his years. He knew that Buck was just another notch on his momma's belt and like some of the other men, he probably wouldn't stay in the picture long enough for him even to learn his last name.

"Hey, lil' man. What's happening?" Buck asked Wayne as Gloria introduced the two of them. "What kind of candy you like?"

Wayne just stood there in the doorway next to his mother. He had heard that question plenty of times; always the same words, different nigga. Wayne almost answered Buck before he even asked the question. The words seemed to fall out of his mouth; he sounded like a broken record. "Any kind," Wayne replied, putting his head down. His mother smiled and patted him on the head like he was a six-year-old child.

"Ain't he so cute?" she said as if she were trying to convince someone in the pet store to buy the runt of the litter. "He's quiet, but he's a good boy. He ain't like all them other little nappy-headed niggas you see running around here, not going to school and things. My boy goes to school. He's gonna be a doctor someday."

Where in the fuck did she get that idea? Wayne thought to himself.

Buck was staring down at Gloria, but he didn't hear a word she was saying. All he saw were her lips moving and a pair of nice round titties. Buck's plan was to send the lil' man to the store to buy some candy so he could taste his mother's candy. Wayne had seen the look Buck was giving his mother several times before. Same look, different nigga.

"Too much candy will make your teeth fall out," Buck said, addressing his comment to Wayne but continuing to eye Gloria while licking his lips. "But sometimes it tastes so sweet it's worth the sacrifice, wouldn't you say, son?"

From that point on, Buck never looked at Wayne again, even when he was addressing him. Instead, he stared at his momma with lust in his eyes. All smiles, Gloria seemed to be taken with Buck. Wayne had decided from the beginning that he wasn't going to say too much to the man. After all, why should he start up a relationship with someone who would soon be replaced by the next man anyhow?

Buck loved running up in Gloria in the backseat of his 1988 Jeep Cherokee. That was usually what their dates consisted of, if they could be called that. Gloria would usually meet him at the construction site where he worked the graveyard shift, down on Wall Street. She would be his midnight snack. And the sex never cost him much either, just a few dollars here and there. Gloria would usually get a bag or two of groceries out of the deal. Since she wasn't a begging, greedy ho, acting like her pussy was lined in gold, Buck decided that perhaps seeing her on the regular and tolerating her kid would be worth it. He reasoned that if the lil' nigga was going to be around, they should at least have some type of understanding. And Buck was well aware that the best way to get on a kid's good side was to bribe him with money or candy. Since he wasn't trying to cough up much more loot, he went with the candy.

Wayne didn't answer Buck. He just stared at him, sizing up the man he knew wasn't going to stick around until his next birthday. He was young, but he wasn't young enough to be bought off with candy. If Buck really wanted to get in good he should have offered him money. Wayne knew the rules to the game his mother played with these men, but Buck was by far the ugliest man he'd seen to date. He felt that if his mother was going to take part in the game, she should at least go after a suave-looking cat, easier on the eyes.

Buck stood there, still staring at Gloria as he reached into his pocket for his wallet. He pulled out a dollar. "Run on down to the store and get you some candy, son. Eat it out there on the stoop." Buck held the money out for Wayne, but Wayne didn't take it.

I should stuff that dollar down your fucking throat, Wayne thought.

"What's wrong, son? You don't like candy after all?" Buck asked. Wayne was silent.

"Of course he does," Gloria answered for Wayne, whacking him on the back of his head. "Boy, you answer people when they talk to you." Gloria turned her attention back to Buck. "He knows better than to ignore people. He just gets a little shy sometimes. He's a good boy, though."

"That's all right, Gloria," Buck said, running his fingers down her cheek. "If the lil' nigga don't want to talk, forget it." Buck knew right then and there that Wayne had peeped game. That shit was going to be a problem and he didn't like it one bit. "I just guess you one of the few kids who don't like candy," Buck bent down to look Wayne in his eyes, "because if you did you'd be takin' this here dollar and going to get you some." Wayne remained silent.

"Boy, you open your mouth and answer Buck or I'm gonna whip yo' ass!" Gloria warned. Wayne's young body shook with rage. At that moment, he could have killed both Buck *and* his mother. She was forcing him to humble himself for the love of a man and his pockets. Wayne felt as if his dignity was being stripped away from him, right along with his mother's.

"Yes sir, Mr. Buck," Wayne growled underneath his breath, trying to hold back the well of tears. "I like Now and Laters."

"What'cha say, lil' man?" Buck asked triumphantly.

"Now and Laters," Wayne said, tightening his lips and wiping his eye with the collar of his tattered British Knights T-shirt.

"Now was that so hard?" Bucked laughed mockingly. "Here ya go, lil' nigga. Take it." Buck handed Wayne the dollar. "Now go on down to the store and get you some Now and Laters and a bag of Bon-Tons. And take yo' time, 'cause me and ya momma here got some business to discuss." He winked at Gloria.

Buck had one hell of an itch going on and wanted Wayne out of his hair so that he could scratch it. After giving Wayne the dollar he opened the door, hinting for him to get to steppin'. Wayne threw on his jean jacket, grabbed his scully from off the television, pulled it over his peasy head, and left.

Immediately, Buck locked the door behind him, figuring that if Wayne couldn't get back in, he couldn't interrupt his and Gloria's groove. With Gloria's ripe body clouding Buck's brain, it never dawned on him to make sure that the back door was locked also. Gloria looked at Buck as he smiled menacingly at her. She didn't really like the way he had brushed Wayne off, but she figured it was better for him to be the bad guy than her. Still, Wayne was a smart kid; he could plainly see that Gloria was an accomplice to the bad guy.

Wayne was no different from other youngsters in similar surroundings. Like most kids in the hood, he had no childhood. He was wise enough to know that it wasn't what Buck was saying that made him the bad guy; it was what his mother wasn't saying. She kept her mouth shut out of fear of saying something that could make Buck leave. The fear of him leaving and taking his wallet with him was what forced her to go along with whatever he put down.

Once the youngster was gone, Buck wasted no time jumping on Gloria. He pushed her up against the door and lifted her knee-length dress over her head. Tearing off her dingy, off-white bra, he began to suck aggressively on her huge brown nipples.

"Slow down, baby," Gloria said, trying to dodge the hot, wet kisses he began burning her neck up with. "We got plenty of time."

"Unh, uh," he said as he continued to grope her body. Buck was far too anxious to get it poppin'. He didn't even bother to remove her panties. He just pulled them to the side and rammed his crooked dick into her.

Gloria attempted to scream out in pain from the sudden penetration. Buck hadn't even gotten her wet yet. He managed to cover her mouth with his hand as he pressed his body up against hers to balance himself. He humped her and began growling like a bear, slobber running down the sides of his big lips as he tried to swallow her tongue. Gloria thought she was going to throw up from the taste of his stink breath.

Holding her breath, she continued to let Buck fuck her in the hallway. She knew he was about to cum by the way his growl was getting louder and louder. She looked at his face and saw that it had become grossly twisted. He was cumming inside of her.

Gloria relaxed her body, let out a sigh, and bent over to pick her dress up from the floor. She was relieved that it was over so quickly. But Buck was no one-minute man. Gloria soon found this out when he took her by the hand and told her to go to the bedroom. Once in the room, he pushed her down to the bed and started to hammer away, not noticing that his roughness had made her start to bleed a little. He just kept grunting and pumping away like a wild animal. Tears ran down Gloria's face as she prayed for him to finish fucking her and just get the hell out, but not without leaving a few ends first.

Meanwhile, Wayne had walked down the block, letting tears flow freely down his chocolate face. He tried to hold them in, but as he walked to the candy store he just couldn't. He didn't mind crying, but he didn't want that fat bastard to know that he had gotten to him. On top of that, he was sick of the abuse that his mother brought on herself and forced him to put up with.

Checking out the neighborhood, Wayne spotted some dude parked in a shiny, cream-colored Cadillac across the street. He was puffing on a cigarette and a couple of nice-looking honeys were leaning on the driver's door hollering at him. He looked like a slick muthafucka. Down the block, four young hustlers were dressed in bomb-ass Adidas, Troop and Gucci suits, and the latest Air Jordans and Reeboks, showing off their whips.

If only I was old enough, I could get out on my own and make a life for myself, Wayne thought. *I could have a nice ride and clothes, too.* And with any luck, Wayne thought, he could do something for his mother.

Wayne approached the store and saw a dirty drunk begging

for money. Everyone just walking by, ignoring him. He was only a reminder of where they really were. All of Wayne's hopes that he thought about on the way to the store had vanished. He felt stuck; he felt unloved.

Upon walking past the drunken bum, he nodded to a few of the neighborhood boys he knew, who were standing across the street, and ducked into the corner bodega. He grabbed a pack of Now and Laters, Lemonheads, and Sour Patch Kids. While the clerk got Wayne's change from the cash register, Wayne snatched up two loose cigarettes from a box on the counter and cupped them in his hand.

"Have nice day," said Carlos in his thick Spanish accent. Wayne nodded back and slipped out of the store with a brown bag full of candy and two cigarettes hidden in the fold of his scully.

Looking up at the sun shining brightly in the sky, he blocked his eyes with his hand and thought about the power of the sun. Up until that point, he had never even noticed it. As far as he was concerned, the sun didn't shine in the ghetto. But today he did notice it, and it seemed happy. It appeared to be smiling at him as if it knew something that he didn't. Wayne suddenly felt a sense of hope. He looked over at the bum, who everybody pretended not to notice. He jingled his change from the store, handed it to the bum, and walked away.

After approaching the group of boys he'd nodded to on his way into the store, Wayne managed to cop a book of matches from one of them. Niggas in the hood could always be counted on to have at least one of three things: a knife, just in case they had to cut a nigga's shit up; a gun, just in case they had to shoot a nigga's shit up; or a light, just in case they had to burn a nigga's shit up.

Wayne decided to take the back streets to his house so that he could smoke his cigarette without some nosy-ass neighbor running back and telling his moms. That would've just given her something else to knock him upside the head for.

The kids on the block would sometimes give Wayne hell about his mother's sexual habits, and he always found himself having to go head up with one of them. Wayne's size had always put him at a hell of a disadvantage. At the age of fifteen, he didn't look like the average fifteen-year-old boy in the neighborhood. He looked about twelve years old compared to them. Nonetheless, he would never back away from a beef.

Once Wayne could see his apartment building from the back alley, he took a few last puffs and stomped out the cigarette with his foot. Climbing up the old fire escape to the back door, he figured he'd been gone long enough for Buck to have finished tagging his mother and be on his merry way. He didn't see or hear anyone, so he assumed that his mother and her company had left. Wayne breathed a sigh of relief at the idea of being alone. He decided to watch television and figure out what to do with the rest of his Saturday.

He plopped down on the old plaid couch in the living room and searched for the pliers to turn on the old floor-model television. Just then, Wayne remembered that the TV had gone out a few weeks earlier. Sometimes his mother let him carry the little thirteen-inch set out of her room and set it on top of the broken one to watch. But Wayne wasn't in the mood to lug that thing from the back of the apartment, so he decided that he would just chill up in his mother's room, eat his candy and watch television there. Wayne took the Now and Laters out and headed to her room. When he got to her closed bedroom door he unwrapped a piece, popped it in his mouth, and proceeded into the room.

As soon as Wayne opened the door, he spit the candy onto the floor. All he saw was his mother on the bed on all fours and Buck's big, fat, naked ass behind her, slamming into her as she held her ass high. Wayne's eyes welled up with tears at the sight of a man hitting his mother doggy-style, as if she were a dog . . . a female dog . . . a bitch. Then the scene got worse. Wayne watched in shock as Buck pulled his penis out of Gloria, turned her around, and busted all over her chest and face.

"Ma," Wayne said in a nervous whisper.

Gloria jumped up and tried to cover herself. She tried hopelessly to wipe the semen off her face. She thought she'd die of shame as Buck grabbed one end of the sheet and began to wipe his dick off with it as if it were nothing but a thang.

"Wayne!" Gloria said, wrapping the sheet around her. "Wayne, baby, I know what it looks like, but momma was just—"

"No sense in sugarcoating it," Buck said, getting up off of the bed and putting on his pants. "The boy's got eyes. He might be young but he ain't blind, or all the way dumb for that matter. He knows what his momma's up to. Probably got him a lil' tender of his own, with all these fast-ass little girls running around here. Don't ya, boy?"

Wayne gritted his teeth and remained silent.

"You probably be doing to those little girls just what I was doing to your momma here, huh? 'Cept y'all probably keep y'all's clothes on, huh?" Buck laughed as he buckled his belt and pulled his wallet out of his pants pocket.

"Be quiet, Buck!" Gloria snapped. "This is between me and my son. Just get the hell out and I'll call you later."

"So it's like that?" Buck asked, getting angry as he snatched up his shirt from the floor. "Ain't I the one that gave you grocery money the other day? You couldn't wait to get me up in this piss hole, and now, just because this muthafucka sees his cunt of a mother for what she really is, I gotta go? You know what? Fuck you and this lil' nappy-headed nigga."

"What?" Gloria squinted her eyes. "Fuck my son? No, you fat, nasty fucker, fuck you! Get the hell out of my house, you fat bastard!"

Buck didn't take well to women ordering him around and calling him out of his name. He had to show Gloria what happened to women who disrespected him, especially cheap-ass tricks like her.

Buck nodded his head; he was plotting. He looked inside his wallet and pulled out a wad of money, just to tease Gloria with. "Fuck me?" he laughed. "Naw, fuck you, you broke-ass bitch. Let's see how fat I am when you and ya little bastard's ribs start rubbing together. I'm getting the hell out of here, all right." Buck pulled his shirt down over his head and slipped on his shoes. "I might be fat, but so is my wallet." Buck closed his wallet up and put it back into his pocket, letting Gloria know that he wasn't giving her a goddamn dime. He then walked out of the room, knocking Wayne to the floor.

"You son of a bitch!" Gloria yelled as she got off the bed and followed behind Buck. "You get back here. You know I need some money."

"You gonna have to learn to respect me," Buck said, heading toward the door. "Now, if you stop while you're ahead, I just might come back and let you try to earn your keep again. But this time, you done gone and let your mouth fuck it up for you."

"Fuck you!" Gloria screamed, chasing behind Buck as he walked out the apartment door. She tripped over the sheet and fell down the outside hallway stairs. She landed at the bottom of the landing, butt naked.

"Don't you leave without giving me some fucking dough!" she screamed. Tears of anger flowed down her face. She had just allowed this man to fuck and nut up inside of her, all in the name of the almighty dollar. And now here he was trying to eat and run.

Buck grabbed Gloria by the arm, dragged her back up the stairs, and flung her into the apartment, where Wayne was standing holding the door open. Wayne picked up his basketball, which was the nearest object, and hurled it at Buck as hard as he could. The ball hit him square in the face. Buck grabbed for his face as blood squirted from his nose.

"You little muthafucka," he said, wiping his bloody nose with his shirt. Buck took off toward Wayne, expecting him to try to run from him. To Buck's surprise, Wayne held his ground. Though it was a noble effort, Wayne was no match for the grown, fat man. Buck hit him in the chest, folding him.

Gloria managed to make her way to the kitchen and pulled out the entire silverware drawer, going for a knife. She knew she had to do something or Buck would kill Wayne.

She darted from the kitchen and ran toward Buck, who was on top of Wayne, choking the life out of him.

"I'm gonna kill you, muthafucka!" Gloria yelled. "Get away from my son."

Buck stood up and was able to restrain Gloria by her wrists, forcing her to drop the knife and the sheet. He let go of Gloria and hauled off and slapped the holy shit out of her, leaving his handprint on her face.

Wayne, still gasping for air, watched helplessly as his mother was brutally beaten. He'd been bullied his entire life, and now he lay there, watching his mother be bullied too. He wished he had a gun. That would even the playing field for sure. He hated the fact that he couldn't protect his mother or himself. At that very moment, he promised himself that once he got a piece, he'd never be caught without it. He would fear no man.

Buck stood over Gloria and laughed.

"Like I said, fuck you, bitch." Buck snorted the blood and mucus from his nose, bringing it to his throat. He hacked it up and spat in Gloria's face. "Punk muthafucka," he mumbled as he looked over at Wayne before heading out the door.

Butt naked, bruised, and starting to swell up, Gloria crawled over to her son and tried to comfort him. "I'm so sorry," she cried. "Oh, my baby, I'm so sorry."

Gloria tried to put her arms around Wayne but he pushed her away. The damage had already been done and Wayne began to rot from the inside. Hate consumed his being, and it was quickly growing like a cancer. He had no intentions of going out like that.

Wayne got up and walked out the door, leaving his sobbing mother behind. He had to start putting together a plan. Fuck waiting until he got older. His time was now.

CHAPTER 4

Nasty Girls

"I NEED SOME LOOT," Crystal said, plopping down on her mother's plastic-covered sofa next to Tonette. Spring was on its way out the door and summer was around the corner. All of the girls were at Crystal's house shooting the breeze, which is what they usually did when their pockets were short. When a bitch didn't have no cash, she sure had conversation. "I'm tired of sitting around this house lookin' at you hoes," Crystal continued. "I wanna go out, but hell, I'm broke. I ain't heard from Dink in two days, so I can't even get nothing from him. I hate not having ends."

"You ain't never lied." Monique, who was lounging in the wicker Huey P. Newton chair, agreed. "A sista's pockets are tight." She leaned forward and squeezed her hands down into the back pockets of her size-eight jeans. She knew she wore a size twelve all day long.

Monique wasn't one of those chicks in denial about her weight. Truth was, most of the hottest designers of the day didn't make clothes that were her real size and she wouldn't dare wear men's jeans. A little discomfort served as her motivation to lose weight. However, if she didn't hurry up and lose some, she was going to end up with chronic yeast infections from wearing her tight-ass Used jeans. She wasn't fat—just plain ghetto-girl thick. She was a pretty brown-skinned girl. Her trademark was her huge gold, shoulder-length, box braid extensions with the burnt ends that she always wore in a high ponytail. She liked to think she was the freshest of all the girls, overcompensating for the fact that Tonette and Crystal were slim, trim, and fly. They always rolled with the niggas with loot, while Monique would travel all the way to Brooklyn to boost clothes, come back home, and say some dude bought them for her.

"Damn, I know all of us bitches ain't broke," Tonette said. "Yo, Crystal, you ain't get *no* money from Dink?" Tonette put her hands on her hips.

"G-i-r-r-rl, did you not just hear me say that I ain't seen or heard from that nigga in two days?" Crystal said, rolling her eyes. "What about you?" she flipped the question on Tonette. "I know you juicin' Dame's hustling ass."

Tonette rolled her eyes. "Crystal, you know Dame's scrooge-ass," she said in disgust. "That nigga got me ridin' the bus. And you know the South Bronx Bitches don't take the fucking bus." Crystal gave Tonette dap.

"Well, all my extra money goes to my son," Shaunna said, jumping into the conversation as she entered the living room from the bathroom. She waved her chipped fingernails, trying to remember the last time she had a manicure. That definitely wasn't like Shaunna, with her wanna-be-diva attitude. Pregnant with her second child, Shaunna waddled over to the rest of the girls, pulling her spandex pants up over her belly.

Coming up, Shaunna Parker had never had it easy. Her mother and father died in a car accident, leaving her to be raised by an uncaring grandmother. Shaunna's grandmother never approved of her son's wife, something she took out on Shaunna regularly. Getting up in age, her grandmother became sickly and had to loosen the noose on Shaunna. Three years ago, Shaunna befriended Tonette, who'd embraced her and added her to the crew.

Together the girls made it their business to be at all the hot spots, including clubs like The Rooftop, 1018, and the infamous disco/skating rink, Skate Key. Quite a few hustlers had always wanted a taste of the pretty, young thick girl from around the way. Shaunna made sure that nearly all of them got a sample of what she had to offer, but only if their paper was long enough.

Shaunna was big-boned. She was a little bigger than Monique but shapelier. Though not nearly as attractive as the rest of the girls, she had an attitude that seemed to ooze sex. She once had a bet with them to see how many dudes she could give blue balls to one night at the club—and she'd won with seven. Shaunna wore a 46-DD and stilled managed to rock bra-and-bikini-panty sets. She would give the average skinny bitch a run for her money any day. As a result of interacting with these hustlers and pimps, she'd acquired a taste for the finer things in life.

She thought that by the way she was moving, she was gaining popularity and prestige, but she was really developing a reputation. After most of the dough-getters in the Bronx (as well as ballers from other parts of New York) knocked the bottom out of young Shaunna's pussy, she had become old news. By the time Shaunna had turned sixteen, she was a high school dropout, pregnant, and on welfare.

"And any other dime I get," Shaunna continued, sitting down

on the love seat next to Laci, "is going to go for shit for this new baby." She rubbed her six-months-pregnant belly.

"And that's exactly why you should have your own money," Laci preached. Her big brown eyes swept the room, looking for one of the girls to back her statement.

"Bitch, please. You get all your money from Mommy and Daddy!" Monique snapped, not appreciating how Laci was shitting on them. When Monique became angry or animated about something, her large nostrils flared like those of a bull seeing red. "Don't even try to front like you do for yourself. I hate it when you do that shit, Laci. We ain't all got parents feedin' us money like you do."

"Monique's right," Shaunna said to Laci, poking out her lips and bobbing her neck. "You always tryin' to make us feel like we nobodies, like we just some fuckin' squirrels runnin' around in your goddamn world, tryin' to get a nut."

Laci just sat there, silent. For the life of her, she couldn't figure out why the girls acted like they adored her at times, but then turned around and showed her nothing but contempt and jealousy. This hurt Laci, because she loved them. These girls were the sisters she'd never had. It was no secret that Laci was definitely the most beautiful and flyest out of the crew. Guys always tried to holla at Laci first, not only because she had a sophisticated, good-girl aura about her, but also because she was the only one out of the crew who didn't have a known reputation.

"You know what, Laci? Forget about your parents," Crystal said, standing up and walking over to her. "What I really want to know is how come I ain't never seen you with no dudes. You don't even *talk* about no dudes, and when they try to mack, you never give them no play. What's up with that?" Crystal asked, puckering her lips and getting right up in Laci's face as if she were conducting an interview. Once one person started in on Laci, it was an open invitation for the others.

"Crystal," Monique said with a disapproving look on her face.

"Crystal, nothing," Crystal continued, rolling her eyes. "Don't act like y'all ain't never thought about it either. So, tell us, Laci, if you don't like dudes, then what *is* your flavor?" Crystal tauntingly twirled one of Laci's curls around her finger.

"I'm more of a private person," Laci said, grabbing her hair from Crystal's fingers and turning away.

"What you mean 'private'?" Tonette quickly cut in, glaring at Laci.

"She means she's a down-low ho," Crystal said. She and the rest of the girls began to laugh. Crystal went and sat back down.

Not finding a damn thing funny, Laci responded. "Private, you know? I don't put my business all out in the streets. It's not ladylike to be running around spreading news about what you do. That's how girls get reputations."

"So what the fuck you trying to say?" Shaunna said, taking offense. "You trying to say we got reps?"

"Yeah," Crystal said, jumping in without hesitation. "Say the shit."

"You sayin' we ain't ladies?" Shaunna asked with major attitude.

"No, Shaunna," Laci said nervously. "Crystal asked me a question and I answered it."

Crystal folded her arms, ran her tongue inside her jaw, and looked over at Tonette. She had a *"should we let this shit ride?"* look written all over her face. Tonette nodded her head in the affirmative. It was better to fall back for a minute before tempers flared and Laci got her long-overdue beat-down.

"This shit is crazy," Shaunna said, looking over at Laci. "This ain't even about you, Laci. Let's keep it real. This shit is about us being a group of young, fine, broke-ass females."

"Uh, huh." Monique popped her bubble gum and nodded her head.

"What the deal with the so-called men in our lives?" Shaunna continued. "We mad at Laci because she ain't dealing with none of these sorry niggas around here. They quick to take some ass but slow on givin' cash. Fuck that!"

"They ain't shit," Tonette said, getting halfway up off the couch. She reached out and gave Shaunna a high-five.

"Most of these niggas ain't worth the sperm it took to get 'em here," Monique added. "It's all well and good when they're cracking for the pussy, but when a sista asks for some cheddar, they start acting all crazy."

"But at the end of the day," Tonette said in all seriousness, "we the ones fuckin' *loco*. We crazy for lettin' them fools get away with it. Them niggas ain't gon' do no more than we allow them to."

"They still triflin'," Monique said, rolling her eyes.

"Yeah, but some of them make up for it in other ways," Crystal said, winking with a sly grin on her face.

Tonette sighed. "There you go thinking with that stankin' pussy of yours again," she said, faking disgust. "Bitch, your whole life is a nonstop fuck fest. I don't even know why you call Dink your man. Everybody know you ain't no one-nigga ho."

"Tonette, you need to quit frontin', actin' like you some goddamn Virgin Mary or some shit," Crystal retorted. "Your pussy is just as raggedy as the rest of ours." Monique and Shaunna snickered. "It ain't my fault that the sorry-ass niggas y'all fuck wit' ain't puttin' it down," Crystal said, adjusting her name belt. "No, Dink ain't the best dick I ever had, but he's my man and he pleases me every time." Crystal was pretty, dressed to def, and had a subtle sexiness in her tall, slender frame. She was daring—wore ripped-up jeans with bright-colored biking shorts underneath and "Yo Baby, Yo Baby, Yo" T-shirts that hung off her smooth shoulders. Her caramel complexion was complimented by the bright blond streaks and asymmetrical mushroom haircut she fashioned after her favorite girl rap group, Salt-N-Pepa.

"Please," Shaunna said, snaking her neck. "My son's father had that good wood, but that don't mean his ass is off the hook financially. Like homeboy said in that movie, '*fuck you, pay me*.'"

All the girls fell out laughing at Shaunna's crazy ass. Shaunna was the oddball of the posse. She was always saying or doing something that would make people ask, "What the fuck?"

"Dink ain't the biggest baller, but his pockets stay laced. You hoes can pop all the shit y'all want to," Crystal said, folding her arms. "A nigga wit' deep pockets is worth his weight, but a nigga wit' a deep stroke is priceless."

"Let you tell it," Laci mumbled in disagreement. Who was she to talk? She was the last virgin in her senior class, and she'd never even used a tampon before. If Laci's parents had taught her anything at all, it was to respect herself, and more importantly, her body. Being the good girl she was, she listened to their words.

"I'm wit' cha on that one, Laci," Monique said. "I can't see no dick being worth more than money."

"That's because you ain't had the right dick," Crystal stated. "I can remember this one dude." She began fanning her private area. "Mercy, mercy me!"

"Shit, don't stop there," Tonette said, turned on by all the dirty talk. "Do tell."

"Go 'head wit' that," Crystal blushed. "Don't nobody wanna hear my story."

"Bullshit," Shaunna said, sitting up to pay attention. "Go ahead, Crystal. Tell us about this so-called stud of yours."

"Yeah," Monique added. "Shit, now I wanna hear about it too."

By now, all of the girls, with the exception of Laci, were on the edge of their wet seats in anticipation of Crystal's sex tale.

"All of y'all nasty," Laci giggled.

"Bitch, please," Shaunna said, sucking her teeth. "You probably got more fuck stories than any of us, wit' yo' prep-school ass."

Shaunna couldn't have been any farther from the truth. Laci was as fresh as a cherry on the vine. As a matter of fact, hers had never even come close to being picked.

"I do not," Laci said defensively.

"Don't even front, ho," Monique said, twisting up her lips. "Come on, tell the truth, Laci. You a closet freak, ain't you, ma? Come on, girl. I know you be around all them young rich white yuppies at your mother's country club."

Laci gave Monique a blank stare. "Whatever," she said, not feeding into Monique's trap. She knew that Monique just wanted to provoke her into saying something, even if it was a lie, but she wasn't falling for it.

"So, what up, Crystal?" Tonette said, eagerly getting back to the subject. "Ain't nobody forgot about your ass. Get to tellin' the story, you little tramp."

"Damn," Crystal said with a smirk. "You all up in my mix." She paused, and a mischievous grin covered her face. "Okay, already. I'll tell the story since y'all ain't gon' let a ho be."

What started out as a boring Saturday night was about to turn into a XXX-rated girl talk session. While Crystal prepared to start, each girl was thinking of what pornographic tale she wanted to share herself.

"And we want full explicit details," Shaunna said, rubbing her stomach. She always enjoyed Crystal's fuck stories, and Crystal enjoyed fucking in order to provide them. Crystal had plenty of them to satisfy Shaunna's appetite. The other girls enjoyed Crystal's sex tales as well, but Shaunna was one of those chicks who really got off on listening to other people's sexual encounters. There was no shame in her game when it came to the flesh. The stories were inspirational and motivational, giving her ideas and perhaps a few tips when it came to her own sexual encounters. The song "Freaks Come Out at Night" by Whodini seemed to be about Shaunna. She would swing episodes with men, women, or both at the same time depending on her mood.

"Aiight, aiight," Crystal began to confess. "His name was Maurice."

"Maurice!" everyone yelled in unison.

"Maurice? What kind of name is that?" Monique asked. "I thought you was gonna say something like Chico or Man or something."

"You know," Shaunna said, "I'm trying to hear some thug passion. He ain't have no street name?"

"Shhh. Just let her tell her story," Tonette ordered.

"Yeah," Laci added, forgetting that she wasn't supposed to be interested in such conversations.

"Now, if there are no further interruptions," Crystal continued, clearing her throat. "I hadn't seen Maurice in a while when I ran into him at the store. I was in the back getting a soda and I see him knelt down reaching for a Colt .45. My pussy got wet at just the sight of him. He and I had kicked it a few times, but the last time I'd kicked it with him and we were about to fuck, his pager went off. He jumped up and said that he had to go take care of some urgent business. He was pissed, 'cause he had eaten my pussy out and was about to get his payback. But anyway, the next time we bumped heads we were still feeling each other. The fact that we only got to see each other in spurts only made it worse. See, Maurice was married."

"Crystal, you messed with a married man?" Laci asked, shocked.

"Damn right," Crystal answered. "I looked at his dick and it didn't have nobody's name on it so I said fuck it. Then that's exactly what I did."

"You know," Monique said, reaching over and giving Crystal five on the black-hand side.

"Besides," Crystal said, "it wasn't my fault that his wife's shit wasn't tight. Plus, Maurice had that good dick. That's why I was just as pissed off as he was that we didn't get to finish up where we had left off. I knew how good that nigga could handle his little dude, or should I say big dude. G-i-r-r-r-l, I had lust in my eyes and larceny in my heart. The two of us were horny just thinkin' 'bout it. We didn't even waste time trying to find a hotel."

"You didn't fuck him in the store?" Shaunna's mouth dropped open.

"Girl, no," Crystal said. "Not that I wouldn't have. That nigga could have slammed me up against the cooler door and fucked the shit out of me, leaving my ass prints on the glass for days."

"I heard that shit," Monique said, crossing her legs, trying to hide the throbbing in the crotch of her pants.

"He drove over to the abandoned houses on 225th," Crystal continued with a smile on her face as she reminisced about her and Maurice handling their business in broad daylight behind a boarded-up tenement building. "That nigga massaged my pussy the whole way there. The bulge in his pants was rock hard. Now I know why niggas startin' to bust sags with they jeans." Crystal wiggled her ass into a more comfortable position as she continued. "Once we parked, he got a blanket from the back of his Jeep and led me over to an old mattress. Maurice laid the blanket out, sat on it, and pulled me down next to him." Crystal paused to fan herself with her hand.

"Come on, bitch," Tonette said playfully, "finish the damn story already."

"You know," Shaunna said, sighing, "I don't know about any of y'all, but this shit is making me . . . oooh!" Shaunna moaned and rubbed her inner thighs. Every time the girls talked about sex, Shaunna would get excited. On a couple of occasions, she actually slid her hand down inside her panties and took care of herself with them all sitting right there.

"How you over there horny with your pregnant self?" Laci asked jokingly.

"Girl, pregnant chicks like to fuck too." Shaunna shot them an *"I thought you knew"* look. "Pregnant pussy is the best. This shit be ripe."

"Let her finish," Monique said, putting her index finger over her lips. Everyone drew their attention back to Crystal.

"I was wearing my purple denim dress, and lifted it up above my hips. Maurice got on top, spread my legs, and pushed my panties to the side. That nigga didn't waste time trying to taste it first. I was so wet that you could hear my pussy talking to him when he touched it with the tip of his dick. The tip alone damn near plugged me up. I kid you not when I say homeboy was packin'. His daddy had to be a horse," Crystal said, not realizing that she was squirming. "I wanted to just fuckin' melt when he started teasing me with the head. He took it easy at first. He knew he was packin', and he had probably beaten up many a pussy. Then he plunged that monster shit as far as it could go. That nigga's dick almost split me clear to my ass."

"I know that hurt," Shaunna said, remembering the labor of her nine-pound, eight-ounce son.

"I took it all in like a real bitch," Crystal said proudly. "I squirted so hard that I thought I was going to faint."

"You lying," Laci said in disbelief.

"I wish I was, Laci," Crystal said. "I'm a two-minute sister, please believe it. But unlike a minuteman, I wanted and was good and ready for some more."

"So did you fuck him again?" Shaunna asked eagerly.

"Hell yeah," Crystal said, rolling her eyes. "Maurice turned me over onto my stomach, clamped his hands onto my shoulders, and gave me the *ooh, aah daddy long stroke*," she sang.

"Ooh, aah, daddy long stroke," they all sang in unison.

"He was beatin' that pussy up." Tonette laughed.

"Okay," Crystal agreed. "He literally fucked tears out of my eyes. When he finally busted a nut, that nigga's dick jerked off inside of me like a loose water hose and he fell out in typical nigga fashion."

The girls sighed and relaxed their bodies that had been so tense with ecstasy.

"That was aiight," Shaunna said, fake yawning. "But I don't see the originality of the story."

"That ain't the end," Crystal smiled. "That was only the climax—literally. Now I need to bring y'all down slowly off the high."

"Go ahead then," Shaunna said anxiously.

"I stood to straighten myself up and noticed that we weren't alone," Crystal said.

"Oh no," Laci said, putting her hand over her mouth. "It was his wife, wasn't it?"

"Will you let me tell the damn story, please?" Crystal said, putting her hands on her hips. "No, it wasn't his wife. Anyway, a car was parked a few feet away. Once I focused my eyes, I realized that it was a fuckin' cracker-ass cop. His ass watched the whole thing."

"Shit, did he lock y'all up?" Laci asked, now more interested in the cop than the sex.

"He threatened to, but decided to take a trade instead." Crystal smiled and ran her tongue across her top lip. "I sucked his dick like a porn star, even jerked his shit off on my face. Needless to say, we were let off scot-free!" Crystal wiped her hands as if she had just taken out the trash.

"Crystal, you's a crazy ho," Tonette said, laughing. "You always set things off right. However, I'm gon' bring it up a notch. I hope y'all ready for this one."

Pandora's box was wide open.

CHAPTER 5

Criminal-Minded

As WAYNE HUFFED and puffed down the street, he decided that the first thing he would need was a gun, and he knew of only one place where he might be able to cop one. He was in hot pursuit. Something in him had snapped, and he was now swiftly moving toward becoming a killer. He had never felt this way before. He felt as though he'd received a calling, and it was as loud as thunder.

After four hours, Wayne spotted the cat who he'd been scouring the streets for. He was sitting outside on an apartment stoop talking to some kid. He was a slightly older hustler who Wayne had only heard people refer to by some nickname that seemed to have slipped his mind at the moment. Wayne had seen him around the way plenty of times, but he had never held a conversation with him. The guy had just always given him a *"what up"* nod or some dap whenever he crossed his path. Wayne didn't know much about him, but he was the only person who came to mind. As Wayne neared the stoop, he saw the dealer hand the kid a few dollars and send him on his way. Wayne took a deep breath and mustered up some courage before approaching the dealer.

" 'Sup, yo?" Wayne asked.

"Chillin'," the hustler responded. He expected Wayne to move on like he usually did, but instead he stayed put. The dealer noticed the hunger in Wayne's eyes, and he could tell that he wanted something. He knew the look well, but it was usually from one of the fiends trying to score. "What you doin' sniffin' 'round these streets all by yaself? It ain't no joke out here, kid."

"I need something," Wayne said, staring down at the hustler's huge gold rope chain with the Cadillac medallion and his Coca-Cola jacket.

"Word?" he asked in shock. "I would have never pegged you. You're too young to have a habit. What are you . . . eleven, twelve or something?"

"I'm fifteen," Wayne said, sticking out his chest. "About to be sixteen."

"Oh, so you just a grown-ass man, then, huh?" he said sarcastically as he began to chuckle.

Wayne just stood there with hunger still burning in his eyes. The dealer could easily see that he wasn't in a joking mood.

"So what can I do for you, lil' man? What you need, some coke, rock—"

"It's personal," Wayne said in a hushed tone, cutting him off.

"Shit, it can't be that damn personal if you're running up on a nigga you don't really know. You must want to share it with somebody?" he reasoned. "For real, though. Talk to me, lil' man."

Wayne looked into his eyes and saw genuine concern. Usually dealers ain't give no play to cats they weren't cool with, but this one didn't appear to be nosy. He just wanted to know what had Wayne combing the tough streets with a mean look in his eyes. Wayne took a deep breath and told him an edited version of what had just gone down between him, Buck, and his mother. He told him how Buck had tried to leave them for dead. The fact that he had caught his mom turning a trick and not getting paid was something he didn't feel the need to share.

The dealer listened attentively. He was drawn in by the intensity with which Wayne told his story. Like hearing a rapper sharing his tale on wax, he could feel what Wayne was saying, even though he hadn't experienced it firsthand.

"That's some heavy shit, lil' man." The dealer sighed, sliding his hand down his face, revealing a four-finger ring with the word DINK on it. The glare from the ring made Wayne squint. "Now I can see why you're out here stressin'. So, what now?"

DARYL WAS ONLY two months old when his heroin-addicted mother traded him to a pusher named Bruce for an ounce.

Although Bruce wanted a son, it was for all the wrong reasons. Never having received much paternal nurturing himself, there wasn't much he could pass on to the boy. Instead of a rose, which needs to be nurtured, Daryl became a weed, growing in whichever direction the streets swayed him. But through it all, he was determined to make his own way. By the time he was eighteen, Daryl was sitting on $250,000 of his own scratch and had three cars without a license.

With a pusher for a father and the streets for a mother, it was understandable how Daryl "Dink" Highsmith could be swayed by the lure of the streets. According to him, school and thoughts of the white man's American dream were nothing more than distractions. So what that he'd scored 1440 on the SAT? An education was not going to put clothes on his back, food on his plate, or money in his pocket.

Within four years, he moved up from small-time pimp to minor-league pusher, and eventually he became the man to see. Daryl had made his choice in life and there was no turning back. The South Bronx was pumpin' with hip-hop, drugs, and death at every corner. It was around this time that he met a chick named Crystal, known for her sweet smile and vicious bite. At first he tried to turn her out, but there was something about the fight in her that made him change his mind. That was only the second time in his life he gave someone the benefit of the doubt.

Together, Crystal and Daryl were a fearsome team. She'd count his stacks every night and sometimes collected for him. However, as his love for her grew intense, he decided that she didn't need to be in the streets with him. He sent her back to her mother's house and was determined to help her get her life together, the way he wished someone had done for him.

"I NEED A gat," Wayne said without hesitating.

The dealer laughed. "What you gon' do with a gun?" he asked, not reading between the lines.

"What you think?" Wayne said, sounding a little harsher than he had intended to sound. "I need to be able to protect myself and my moms. A nigga never gonna run up in my crib again. Ya know what I'm saying?"

The dealer took a deep breath and then let out a sigh. "That's a tall order, lil' man," he said, rubbing his hands together. "All kinds of fucked-up shit happens with guns, man. A little dude like yaself might get hurt, or hurt somebody and bring a lot of heat down on the niggas out here serving. The first thing they'll want to know is where you got the piece from."

Wayne wasn't up for reasoning. He could see now that he needed to move on. "Yo, if you don't wanna hook me up, then I'm out!" Wayne held his hand out to give the dealer some dap. He wanted him to know that even though he wasn't going to help him out, they were still cool.

"Hold on, hold on. I didn't say that I didn't want to help you out," the hustler said, grinning. "But this is business." All of a sudden the little compassion he did have was out the window, quickly replaced by the attitude of a cunning businessman. "How you going to pay for what you need, homeboy?"

In Wayne's haste, he'd never thought about that little obstacle. In his quest for revenge, he had forgotten the most common law of the streets: nothing came without a price. This was something that hadn't crossed his mind, but he wouldn't be swayed.

"I ain't got no money," Wayne confessed.

"Then you're shit out of luck," the dealer said, turning his head to look down the block.

This was typical. One minute a muthafucka was up in your corner, and as soon as he found out your pockets were full of lint, he wasn't checking you no more.

"Hold on, man," Wayne said, taking a seat next to him. "Maybe I can work it off?"

"I feel for you and all, but damn, lil' man, this ain't Burger King," the dealer snarled. "I deal in cash, baby. Besides, what the hell can you do? You ain't no drug dealer. You ain't even no mule. You ain't got no street savvy or you wouldn't have ever stepped to me like you did in the first place. I can see your ass fuckin' up the game for everybody, so why should I put you on?"

Wayne thought on it for a minute before speaking. "I can do other things for you. Whatever you need done, if you know what I mean," he said, throwing his hands up humbly. "No need frontin' me a gat if it's no use to you. Point a nigga out, and he's a memory."

The dealer laughed. "That's big talk for a lil' man. But if your heart is as big as your mouth, then we just might be able to work some shit out. Peep this, you don't just wake up one morning and decide that you want to be a killer. It don't work like that. Besides, that don't even seem like ya style. You need to have yo' lil' ass in school or something."

"You don't know me, it *is* my style, and fuck school. Going to school might mean a nigga can survive working for the man, but it don't teach nothin' about surviving in these streets. I'm tired of getting stepped on. A muthafucka ain't gon' never catch me without something ever again." Wayne spoke angrily, spitting his words.

The vision of his mother crying as Buck spit on her would be permanently etched in his mind, forever. "I'ma eat, sleep, fuck, and take a bath wit' my shit. It's 1987 and I ain't takin' no shorts."

"I don't know, homeboy," the dealer said to Wayne. "Ghostin' somebody ain't easy. You gotta have that shit in your heart. Pulling that trigger is a muthafucka—the power behind it, the pull, the smoke and the heat. A lot of niggas are carrying burners, but everybody ain't busting them, know what I mean? Some of these cats wear their shit around their waist like they makin' a fashion statement. You might just be talking out ya ass because you all pissed off right now."

"I'll tell you what," Wayne said, getting angry. "Hook me up wit' a piece and you can watch me put a nigga's head to bed."

Just then, some girl came heading their way. She was a hottie for sure—dark-skinned, color contacts, goddess braids with her baby hair slicked down and probably styled into waves by a toothbrush. The little bit of makeup she was wearing was just enough, as her skin was as smooth as the leather interior of a Caddy. She was wearing an off-the-shoulder polka-dot shirt, a denim miniskirt that showed off her bowlegs, fishnets, and turquoise pumps.

"Hey, daddy," she said, approaching the dealer.

"Hey, now, baby girl," the dealer replied as he stood up from the stoop and met her a few steps down. "What can I do you for?"

"I know what you like," she said with a wink, "and you know what I like."

"I'm straight on that stuff," the dealer said, turning away from her. "My shorty took care of that for me before I left the crib, so no bartering tonight, baby girl. No cash, no stash."

"I got money," she said, copping that junkie attitude.

"Then we straight," the dealer said, looking around. Then he pulled a pack of Kools from his back pocket and emptied a crack rock into the palm of her hand. Her eyes lit up like she was looking at a gold nugget. Slowly, she slipped her hand down the front of her skirt, placed the rock in the crotch of her panties, and pulled out some money.

"Here you go, daddy," she said, handing him the crumpled-up five-dollar bills. "Take a whiff of that to remind you of me. What I got is better than money and you should never forget it."

"Later," the dealer said, unimpressed. She was a bum, but not like the man outside the bodega. She was a bum to all the dudes in the neighborhood. That was how they referred to old pussy. And there was certainly something better than old pussy—new pussy. Her shit was done.

The girl blew the dealer a kiss, then looked over at Wayne. "Breaking them in younger and younger every day, huh?" she said to the dealer. "He's a little cutie, too. Maybe one day you might wanna do something nice for your little worker bee. You know I'm always willing to work for mine. Later, fellas." She strutted away.

"Sorry about that," the dealer said, stuffing the Kools back in his pocket. "That was just Peaches. Ho will do anything for a rock."

Wayne stood there in awe, watching her walk away. She didn't look anything like the neighborhood crackheads he had seen before. She seemed so sweet and innocent—not to mention fine. No way was she copping that shit for herself.

The dealer observed Wayne staring at the girl until she was out of sight. "Looky here," he said, laughing. "Lil' man diggin' on Peaches. Man, she's gotta be twice your age. How old did you say you were again?"

"Why?" Wayne snapped, not appreciating being laughed at. "Is that gon' make a difference in whether you let me hold something?"

"You really is a hard lil' nigga, huh? I see the potential. I like your heart and I just may have some work for you. But I don't even know your name, homebody."

"It's Wayne."

"Wayne . . . Wayne what?"

"Just Wayne," he said, figuring that was all the dude needed to know for now, unless he decided to help him out for certain.

"Okay, tough guy," the dealer teased. "You sure don't look like no Wayne. With that scully sitting on top of ya head like that, you look like a black-ass Smurf. And you kinda act like the little angry one. Matter of fact, fuck that *Wayne* shit. I'm gonna call you Smurf. That's yo' new name, lil' nigga. Get used to it."

"Whatever," Wayne said, waving him off. "So can I get that piece now or what?"

"What's the hurry, Smurf?"

"I need to take care of some important business. I've already wasted enough time."

"What exactly *is* your business?" the dealer asked, searching his face.

"What kind of business you think?"

"There you go again with that shit. If you gonna be down wit' a nigga, you gotta keep it real. You gotta lay your shit out flat."

"First off," Wayne obliged, "I need to take care of some shit. I want to go ahead and knock down the first domino."

The dealer nodded his head and smiled. He knew Wayne wasn't the street-bred type of cat, but he could tell that he'd seen a lot. And his street finesse seemed to flow naturally. It needed some polishing, but the kid had potential.

"Second off, do you really want me to make you an accessory before the fact?" Wayne said, using the language he had learned from the prime-time law shows like *L.A. Law* and *Columbo.*

"Okay, Smurf," the dealer said with a chuckle. "Follow me."

He led Wayne over to his parked car, a brand-new cherry-red Benz 300 with a spoiler kit. He ordered him to get in on the passenger side, while he opened the driver's door. Inside the car, the hustler opened the glove box and pulled out a brown paper bag. He handed it to Wayne.

Wayne opened the bag and saw a shiny .32. He stroked the pistol inside the bag. He didn't dare pull it out on the Ave. like that. He could feel the hammer singing to him as his finger stroked the metal. He sat there like a deer caught in headlights, admiring the pistol.

"Think you can work with that?" the dealer asked.

"Hell yeah," Wayne said, snapping out of his daze. "I'll bring it right back when I'm done."

"Nah, it's yours now. You keep it. And just remember, if anything happens, forget where you got it."

"Word?" Wayne said, smiling and rocking his head. "Thanks, man, I owe you for real."

"Hell yeah, you owe me, and I plan to collect," the dealer said. "Where you live, yo?"

"I'll connect with you right back here in a couple of days," Wayne said, ignoring the question.

"That's cool. I feel that," the dealer said, smiling at Wayne, who was acting like Santa had just brought him exactly what he had asked for on his Christmas list. "Damn, you do look just like a Smurf."

"I'll be that," Wayne said. "I'll be a Smurf all day long, just as long as I got the heat."

The dealer reached into the backseat and grabbed a book. He began to flip through the pages. "You read, Smurf?"

"Nah," he said, tucking the bag under his shirt.

"You ever heard of the Dutchman?"

"Who?"

"The Dutchman—Lucio Dutch."

"Nah, who is that?"

"Damn, Smurf. You got a lot to learn." The dealer loved to read, and he passed books on to people he knew didn't read but needed to. "Here, read this," he said, handing Wayne the book.

"I want you to read a few pages and tell me what you think the next time I see you."

"I don't want to read no book," Wayne protested. "Ain't nobody got time for all that."

"You ain't got no money for that burner, either," the dealer reminded him. Wayne had no response. "All right then," the dealer continued. "Read a couple of pages and catch up with me."

"Cool," Wayne said, giving him some dap. Wayne opened the car door to exit, but he paused and looked at the dealer. "In case I don't see you around and I need to ask if anyone's seen you, who do I say I'm looking for?"

"The name is Dink. Just mention your name, and they'll know to hit me up. And remember, from this point on you're Smurf, but don't worry; I'll be here. You just show up and tell me about what you read."

"I got it. Don't you worry. Smurf will be here," Wayne said, getting out of the car and closing the door behind him. "Oh yeah, by the way, I didn't just wake up one day and decide that I wanted to be a killer." He paused. "I was born one."

Dink nodded with respect as Smurf walked away.

AFTER COPPING THE piece, Smurf wandered around the hood, hopped the train, and rode it for a couple of hours. Having collected his thoughts and calmed his anger, he headed home to check on his mother and prepared for what he planned on doing with his new gat. As soon as he walked through the door, she threw her arms around him.

"Dammit, boy. Where have you been? It's almost eleven o'clock. I been worried sick. I thought you done ran out here and done something stupid," she said frantically.

"I'm all right, Mom. I didn't do nothin' stupid."

His mother sat him down on the living room couch and tried to continue quizzing him about his whereabouts, but he only fed her lies. Finally she gave up. Smurf sat there and watched her down a bottle of rum. She eventually fell over onto his lap in a drunken sleep.

As she snoozed on the living room couch, Smurf watched her and felt a pain in his heart. He hated to be hard on his mother, but she didn't seem to want it any other way. He promised himself that he'd help her get out of her rut. He wanted to help her more than anything, but he had to help himself first. After staring at her for a few more moments, Smurf slid from underneath her and headed to bed.

Smurf couldn't think straight. He sat up all night in bed staring, holding, polishing, and aiming his new piece. Sunday he damn near did the same thing. The gun was like a new puppy. He couldn't wait to get out of school Monday afternoon to go home and let it out to piss. He daydreamed all day long in school, thinking about putting one through Buck's head. After school he did his homework, ate dinner, and prepared to skip out of the house when his mother went to sleep. Time was of the essence.

Smurf had itched to get at the nigga all weekend, but he decided to wait until Monday, when he thought Buck would more likely be working. Dressed in all black, he tucked his pistol in the front pocket of his hoodie. When he peeked into the living room, there his mother was, drunk and asleep on the couch in the same spot she had been for the past two days. Smurf walked over to her, kissed her on the forehead, and dipped out.

He boarded the Number 2 train and rode it all the way downtown to Wall Street. He had the jitters the entire ride. He thought about turning back, but his conscience wouldn't let him. Buck had violated his home and family. According to the laws of the jungle, he had to be handled.

Finally at his destination, Smurf jogged up the subway stairs, making sure to hold his piece so it wouldn't fall out. Once outside, the night air greeted him. The cool wind against his face was just what he needed. It didn't take him long to locate the construction site. It was the only one on the block. Smurf walked past it, but he made sure to stay on the opposite side of the street. As far as he could see, there was one entrance in the front and another one where deliveries were made on the side. He decided that the latter would be his point of entry.

Smurf crept to a side window and tried to get a good look into the structure. Through the dirty glass, he could see Buck sitting behind a desk watching a small television. As far as Smurf could tell, he was alone. He could climb right through the window and blow his fuckin' brains out without worrying about witnesses, but there was an alarm on the door. Something he hadn't counted on; quick-witted, he thought of a way to use it to his advantage. He pushed against the door, setting the alarm off, and waited.

Within seconds, Buck poked his fat head out the door to investigate. His skin turned stark white at the sight of a pistol pointed at his dome. Smurf smiled at the big man, who looked as if he was about to pass out.

"Back yo' fat ass up," Smurf ordered. Buck nodded and did as he was told. Smurf followed him through the door and secured it behind them. "Guess the tables have turned, huh?"

Buck tried to keep a straight face as he nodded, but his knees wouldn't stop shaking. He'd gotten a thrill out of savagely fucking Gloria and kicking the shit out of her kid, but now he would give anything to change the past.

"Listen, boy," Buck pleaded. "I know you're angry, but—"

"Shut the fuck up!" Smurf ordered. "You don't know how I feel, so don't say another fuckin' word. You ain't so mutha-fuckin' tough now, is you?" Smurf asked with an insane-looking grin. "You felt like a big man when you was hittin' on a woman and a kid, but now you ain't shit . . . fuckin' coward. Why you ain't poppin' that shit now?"

"I didn't mean it," Buck said, crying freely. "Shit just got out of hand. I was angry, man. I didn't mean to hurt you and your moms. I swear to God."

"You lyin' muthafucka!" Smurf screamed, slapping Buck with the gun. Buck crumpled to the ground, holding the side of his head as blood poured from the wound.

Seeing Buck humbled in such a way sent a rush through Smurf. He was the only thing that stood between Buck living and dying. He felt godlike. He felt a surge go from the back of his head and through his arm, eventually moving to his hand, which began to stiffen. Finally, the powerful sensation spread to his finger.

The first shot hit Buck in his chest. Smurf tried to gain control of his hand, but he couldn't. Whatever evil lurked within the firearm had possessed him. His arm jerked over and over, filling Buck's body with lead. Buck's screams mingled with the sound of the barking gun, threatening to drive Smurf mad. When it was all said and done, the only thing that could be heard was the squeaking spring in the gun's hammer.

Smurf stared at Buck's bullet-riddled body and nearly threw up. He forced his dinner to stay down long enough to admire his handiwork. Buck was hit up real ugly, but it was a suitable death for a man who'd done such ugly things. Smurf took a moment to spit on his corpse before disappearing into the night. Tomorrow would be a new day, and he was anxious to see what kind of work his new employer had lined up for him. But little did he know, more than two years later he'd still be putting in work for Dink.

CHAPTER 6

Girl Talk

"ALL RIGHT, ARE you guys ready?" Laci wanted to make sure everyone was listening. She said it as if she was only going to tell the story once, and if you missed it, you missed it.

"I'm on the verge of cummin' in my maternity drawers," Shaunna said, stretching out. "Laci, I hope your story does it for me."

Laci cleared her throat. "I had fallen asleep on the couch at Mark's house."

"Mark?" Monique asked. "Who the fuck is Mark?"

"Just let her tell the goddamn story before you fuck up my nut now, shit," Shaunna's nasty ass said.

Laci continued, "Mark woke me up by eating me out. He flicked his tongue across my clit, blowing it up to the size of a marble. I had never felt that kind of tingling in my body. Mark sent me there."

Laci appeared to be in la-la land. Every girl's face wore the look of surprise. Laci had never spoken like this before. As Laci told her story, for the first time she felt like she was being fully accepted by the girls. It motivated her to continue.

"After Mark made me cum," Laci slid off the couch and onto the floor, "I played with his dick until it got good and hard. I teased him by just licking on the head, but not putting him in my mouth. He begged, but I still wouldn't do it."

"That's right, girl. Make that nigga beg," Monique said, leaning over toward Laci to give her a high-five.

"When Mark's eyes started tearing up, I finally gobbled him up. He was surprised at how much muscle control I had. I opened my throat and took all of him. Now, Mark wasn't very thick, but he was long as hell. I felt like gagging, but I held it down." Laci paused, making sure the girls were still into her story. "I didn't want him to cum in my mouth, so I ended up jumping on top of him and sat on it. He grabbed my ass while he humped me back. I started to lose my mind."

"Ride that dick, Miss Prissy," Tonette chimed in enthusiastically.

Laci smiled and continued. "I came so hard and fast, it felt like someone kicked it out of me. Things just got harder and more violent. He smacked me on the side of my ass—not hard enough to hurt me, but hard enough to make my clit jump. The pain felt so good that I screamed out, 'Hit me harder.' The sound of him smacking my ass pushed me over the edge. That was the first time I had ever cum just by the sound of my ass getting smacked."

Monique pretended to wipe a tear from the corner of her eye. For the first time, she was proud of Laci's yellow ass. Laci could see the excitement in the girls' eyes as she told the story. She couldn't stop there.

"This is kind of embarrassing," Laci said, "but the sensation made me erupt and I . . . I pissed on him. I could've died right there, but Mark seemed to get more turned on."

At this point in the story, Crystal twisted her lips up and had a look of disbelief on her face. She knew that no matter how hard you tried to piss during penetration, you couldn't.

Laci went on telling the story, caught up in her own drama. "He told me to stand up and let my pee run all over his body," Laci said, shrugging her shoulders. "Mark started to squirm and moan under the stream of piss. He blew his wad all over the place. He loved it." At first her story had all the girls horny, but then it got weird. Laci had eight pairs of eyes on her that never once lost focus. She felt compelled to proceed. "So I wiped him with a towel, and then he threw me on the floor and pushed my legs back to my ears. I lay there helpless while Mark dug into my guts. Then, oh my God, he started hitting a spot that I didn't even know I had. I started screaming at the top of my lungs. He knew he was tearing it up, and that excited him so much that he erupted inside of me, rolled over, and passed out. Hell, I thought he might have had a heart attack or something. I started whispering his name. I wanted to tell him how good he had made me feel, but he wouldn't respond. I started nudging him and he wouldn't budge. Fear set in, and I sat up and started rubbing him on his chest while continuing to call his name. Still, he didn't move," Laci said with great intensity, as if she were reading a Stephen King novel to the girls. "His body didn't feel right," she continued. "I began to get nervous, so I checked him for a pulse. Nothing. Mark had died in the pussy. It wasn't until later that I found out he had a bad heart. See, he had been born with some crazy heart condition. You know what I mean?" Laci said in a tone that sounded as if she might have been trying to convince herself as well as the girls.

For a few moments, the room was silent. The girls just sat there looking at each other. Then they looked at Laci. For the first time, the bitches were speechless. It took everything inside of Laci not to bust out laughing, but she couldn't hold it in any longer. Out of nowhere, she started laughing uncontrollably.

"You lying bitch," Monique said as she began to chuckle.

"What?" Laci said, still laughing, but acting like she had no idea what Monique was talking about.

"I don't believe you just fucked up my nut like that," Shaunna said, trying to hold back her laughter, but letting a slight chuckle slip out. "Hell, you actually fucked me up once you started talking about a dead muthafucka. I ain't into hearing about fucking a dead corpse and shit."

The girls all started laughing.

"I'll admit," Crystal said, "Laci, you had me with you in the beginning. You even had me at the golden shower part, but you's a lyin' ho. You know damn well you made all that shit up."

"Psych!" Laci said, pointing.

Tonette picked up one of the plastic-covered pillows from off the couch and threw it at Laci. "I can't believe you," she said. "Had us all caught up. Somebody else could have been talkin' 'bout some real shit."

"You know," Crystal added, "real bitches do real shit."

"My bad, ladies," Laci apologized as she got her laughter under control. "I wanted to be a part of the storytelling for once."

Monique was fed up. "I don't know 'bout y'all hoes, but she ruined the sex shit for me."

"Ditto," Shaunna agreed. "You got some food up in your kitchen, Crystal? My baby is hungry."

"Bitch, *your* fat ass is hungry," Crystal said jokingly. "That baby don't know what the fuck food is."

"I ain't pregnant, but I'm eating for two anyway," Monique said as she stood up and stretched out. "What you got to whip up?"

"I don't know," Crystal said, getting up from off the couch. "Come into the kitchen and see what you have a taste for."

All of the girls followed Crystal into the kitchen.

"What's up for the summer?" Monique asked no one in particular as they entered the kitchen. All the girls looked at each other but said nothing. Monique tried again. "Let's not all answer at the same time," she said sarcastically. "No one has any plans? Tonette, what about you?"

"I ain't really got anything planned," Tonette said, shrugging her shoulders. "Hell, I'm living just enough. You know how I get down. I play it on a daily. I was thinking about maybe trying to take some classes for that stupid-ass GED again."

"Evidently it ain't the GED that's stupid," Laci said, hoping to make a cute joke. She immediately wished she could take it back.

Tonette stopped in her tracks. What she wanted to do was haul off and slap the shit out of Laci, hell, maybe even take one of them butcher knives from the block in Crystal's kitchen and cut her fuckin' throat. But something told her to let it go, and she did. She looked at Laci and forced a fake grin. "Ha, ha. That was real funny, Laci."

Crystal rolled her eyes at Laci, shook her head, and opened the refrigerator door.

"Sorry," Laci said, putting her head down. "I was just kidding. You know I would never come at you like that."

"Yeah, I know," Tonette said insincerely. She told herself to let it go . . . for now anyway. "Crystal," Tonette said, moving on, "what about you? What you got going on for the summer?"

"You know I just want to chill," Crystal answered as she examined the contents of the refrigerator. "But I'm also thinking about summer school. Maybe there won't be as many guys there to distract me." Crystal closed the refrigerator door and opened the freezer.

Monique interjected. "Well, I don't have to worry about a GED, high school diploma, or none of that. I gots my high school certificate of completion."

"You mean attendance, don't you?" Shaunna said jokingly. "You got a certificate for just showing up every day."

"You stupid," Monique said. "I'm getting my high school diploma. I passed the son of a bitch with flying D-minuses." The girls started laughing. "But seriously, if y'all hoes gon' be all caught up wit gettin' an *edumacation*, then maybe I should do the community college thing. Crystal, you trying to go to college someday?"

"Nah, I just want my diploma," Crystal said with a shrug. "Dink said if I get it, he gon' take me out to celebrate anywhere I want to go. You know I'm trying to go to Morton's Steak House."

"I know you glad you got him," Shaunna said. "He be takin' care of you. That's why I don't know why you ever crying broke. You know all you got to do is ask that nigga to hold something and you straight."

"I know," Crystal said, pulling out a block of bologna from the fridge. "But I don't like to always have my hand out. Niggas get tired real quick of a beggin' bitch. If he don't give it to me on his own, I usually only ask him when I really, *really* need to hold something. Y'all want some of this?" she said, holding up the bologna.

"Yeah, fry it up," said Shaunna. "I wish I had a muthafucka holdin' me down like that," she said, reflecting on her own situation. "I wish I'd done my thing in school instead of poppin' babies out by a no-good nigga. Seems like you can't do shit without a diploma."

"Fuck that," Tonette cut in, sounding frustrated. "If I get it, I get it. That shit don't hold no weight for black folks anyhow. Once you get a diploma or GED, muthafuckas start talkin' about you need a bachelor's degree to make some real paper. Then the next thing you know, that ain't even good enough. The system ain't built to work for us."

Monique nodded. "Got a point there. I mean, I think I wanna go to college, but who the hell wants to sit through another four years of school? That shit ain't gon' get me no money. I should probably just get a job at the post office or the bank. They pay three hundred dollars a week. I could get a Fourth of July outfit and new leather Gucci jacket with that."

Laci looked at her friends and shook her head. Monique had no job experience and didn't have the temperament to work for anyone. Besides that, she had too much pride to apply at the places where she was qualified to work. There was no way she was going to get a job at a bank.

"You awful quiet over there," Crystal said to Laci as she sliced the bologna and threw it in the frying pan.

"We already know that bitch probably gon' die in school," Monique laughed. "She's probably going to be one of those career students who as long as they stay in school, Mommy and Daddy will foot the bills."

Laci ignored the comments and said nothing.

"I don't know what I'm gon' do aside from have this baby," Shaunna added. "I know someone in Housing and they supposed to hook me up with a two-bedroom apartment. Hopefully, by the time the baby comes, I'll have more space. But y'all know how the system works. President Reagan don't give a shit about black folks in the hood." Shaunna sighed and rubbed her stomach.

The girls just stood there staring at her, feeling her pain.

"Monique, look in the cabinet and get the red Kool-Aid mix. Y'all want something to drink while I fry this up?" Crystal said to break the monotony.

The girls all nodded or mumbled yes.

"Do you know what you're having?" Laci asked Shaunna.

Shaunna's face lit up. "No, I want to be surprised. I already have my son, so it would be nice to have a girl. But only God knows."

Laci walked over to Shaunna and held her hand up to her stomach. "Can I?" she asked with caution.

"Yeah, go ahead," Shaunna said with surprise in her voice. None of the girls had ever seemed to want to connect with the little life inside of her.

Laci placed her hand on the center of Shaunna's belly and pressed softly. It was an amazing feeling to Laci. Shaunna's belly was as hard as a rock and she could actually feel the baby. It was surreal.

"Who's the father?" Laci asked innocently.

It was like a record had started to skip and the deejay snatched off the needle. There was dead silence. Shaunna disregarded Laci's question and asked one of her own.

"What about you, Laci?" she said, removing Laci's hand from her stomach and walking over to the snack table to retrieve her drink. The other girls followed her lead.

"Yeah, Laci, what are you getting into this summer?" Monique asked. They all looked at her.

Laci's inquisitiveness had set her up for the fall. She didn't know how to answer the question without starting an argument. For some reason, she could never get shit right. She always managed to say the wrong thing. If she told the truth, the girls were going to start trippin' on her. If she didn't tell the truth, they'd know. They were like Superman when it came to Laci; they could see right through her. Her lying to them would only piss them off even more.

"Uh, nothing much. Just going to Puerto Rico before I leave for college," Laci tried to say nonchalantly as if it was no big deal.

Crystal wasn't about to let Laci get off so easy. "Oh, so Little Miss Thing's parents are paying to broaden her education?" she said, batting her eyes and puckering her lips. "Figured as much. Too bad the rest of us don't have caked-up parents."

"First of all, it's just me and my mother—you know that. And, I got a scholarship," Laci said, shutting Crystal up.

"Scholarship?" Monique asked, confused. "You ain't no athlete. I ain't never known you to play ball, run track, or nothing."

Laci shook her head. "I received an academic scholarship," she said as if she were talking to a child.

"Academic?" Monique asked, still a little baffled.

Crystal helped Monique comprehend. "Duh, yeah, stupid," she teased. "When you get good grades, colleges give you a free ride to their school. It ain't like she, of all people, needs it though."

Trying to cover up her jealousy, Tonette joined in on the conversation. "What school are you going to, Laci?"

"Boston University," Laci said proudly.

"That's supposed to be a pretty good school," Shaunna said.

"How the hell would you know?" Monique said, taking a sip of her drink.

"Fuck you, slut," Shaunna shot back. "I had an uncle who went there, so now."

"So now," Monique mocked Shaunna, sticking her tongue out at her.

"You keep playing and I'm gonna put that pretty tongue of yours to use," Shaunna winked.

"Oooh, can I watch?" Crystal joked as she finished up her drink and sat the cup down on the snack table.

"Anyway," Tonette cut in, "forget about that school shit. What's this about Puerto Rico?"

Laci swallowed down her Kool-Aid, hard. The girls looked at each other with a mixture of jealousy and hatred. All of them wished that they could travel anywhere other than the five boroughs, but they weren't as blessed as Laci. The only thing that saved Laci from a round of Bash the Rich Girl was Crystal's boyfriend, Dink, who was standing in the doorway.

CHAPTER 7

Schemin'

DINK COULDN'T TAKE his eyes off of Laci. There was something about her that wouldn't allow him to look away. She was pretty, but not enough to trip over. He had seen pretty girls come and go. This one, though, just had a certain air about her that he couldn't shake. She had his nose open without even trying.

Crystal was his boo-boo, but he wasn't in love with her anymore. If anything, he liked her a lot and had love for her, but as far as being in that unconditional love bullshit, it wasn't happening. When it all came down to it, Dink saw Crystal as not being much different from the rest of her crew. She was okay to look at when she was dressed up, but not wifey material. Laci, on the other hand, had something about her that Dink needed to know more about.

Crystal read Dink's eyes like a kindergarten spelling test. She wasn't the sharpest knife in the drawer, but she was hardly stupid. She knew the look that Dink was giving Laci, because that's exactly how he'd caught her two years ago. The muthafucka could bat his eyes and lick his lips all he wanted, but Crystal was determined to show the both of them who the queen bitch was.

Hugging Dink, she kissed him on the neck. "I think you left something in my room," she whispered loud enough for everyone to hear. For emphasis, she grabbed his package.

"Damn, Crystal," Dink said. He held her at arm's length. There are people here." He fronted like he was embarrassed, but Dink really loved that kind of shit. Crystal was a freak and a half, which was part of the reason he kept her around. He thought about the last time she had sucked him off and let him blow in her mouth. Just thinking about it made Dink want to wet himself.

Crystal and Dink's fooling around made Tonette jealous. It had been a minute since her main nigga, Dame, had given her a taste. She figured if she couldn't get any, she'd block Crystal's action.

"Crystal," Tonette coughed.

"Okay, okay," Crystal giggled. "Y'all know how I get when I see *my* man." Crystal shot a look at Laci, hoping that she understood where she was coming from just in case she had any ideas.

Dink zipped down his Sergio Tacchini sweatsuit jacket and flipped it behind him like Michael Jackson, exposing his Polo shirt and two gold rope chains with a Batman medallion. He was in stunt mode now. "So what you ladies getting into tonight?"

"Nothing really," Shaunna said, rubbing her stomach. "We'll probably keep it local. Besides, I can't go too far with this belly."

"You probably don't need to be going nowhere," Monique said. "Why you always gotta be the pregnant girl at the club?"

The girls snickered. Shaunna stuck her middle finger up at Monique.

"Do you know what it is yet?" Dink asked, walking over to Shaunna and placing his ear against her stomach.

"What the fuck you think you gon' hear?" Crystal said, jealous that Dink was touching Shaunna. "You think it's gonna bust out freestyling or something?"

"I don't know if it's a girl or a boy," Shaunna said, running right over Crystal's comment. "I want to be surprised."

Even though Dink had no intentions for Shaunna, the attention he was giving her made her feel warm. Her own children's fathers didn't pay that kind of attention to her. She wasn't used to it, and this only made her crave it more. As Dink began to rub her stomach, she imagined that he was her man instead of Crystal's.

"That's cool," Dink said, smiling. "Did you eat yet? You know you gotta keep your strength up."

"Damn, baby," Crystal cut in, "since when you love the kids? She's fine, she just ate two fried bologna sandwiches." Crystal walked over to where Shaunna was sitting and pulled at Dink's arm. "C'mon now, I ain't seen you in a minute. I missed you. Shit, nigga, come rub on me."

"I missed you, too," Dink said, patting Crystal on the ass. "You think I don't think about you when I'm out handling my business? C'mon now, you know you're always on my mind. Stop actin' like that."

Dink hugged Crystal and lifted her off her feet, but with her back turned, it meant that he could study his prey—Laci. When Laci realized that Dink was burning a hole through her with his eyes, she blushed and turned her head. She used her tongue to scoop a piece of ice from her cup. Her smile let Dink know that she was finally onto him. And although he was involved with her homey, time and opportunity was a muthafucka. All he needed was an opportunity, and hell, he'd make the time.

Dink released Crystal. "I'll see you girls later," he said, quickly eyeing Laci. "Y'all be safe. Crystal, you go on and have a good time with your girls, ma." He reached in his pocket and pulled out a wad of rolled-up hundred-dollar bills. Each of the girls had her eyes on his cash except for Laci, who knew better than to stare, and Crystal, who was checkin' to see who was sweatin' her man. "I'll be back later to check you out." Dink pulled off eight bills, handed them to Crystal, licked his lips, and shot a quick last glance at Laci. There was no mistaking what his intentions were. This time she didn't turn away or look down. She stared at him right back. Dink nodded and left.

The girls were silent until they were sure he was out the door.

"Dink is a classy-ass nigga," Monique said, picking at her nails. "He fine, too. You better watch him, Crystal. One day one of these loose-ass sluts is gonna try you. You can trust his ass all you want. It's these hoes you can't trust."

Crystal nodded in agreement. Typically it would have struck a nerve for some other female to call her nigga fine. But Monique and Crystal were the tightest, like sisters, so Monique was the only one out of the crew who could make the comments she did without Crystal hitting the roof. The other girls just kept silent and stewed in their own juices, romanticizing the forbidden idea.

Laci looked down at her watch. "Well, ladies, it's been real, but I'm about to bounce," she said, stretching. "I'm gonna go home and lay it down."

Crystal looked over at Tonette; her eyes bulged. Tonette shrugged her shoulders as if to say, *"handle yours."* Then Crystal quickly said, "But Laci, you're always on some leaving shit. You be acting like you're too good to be with us after a certain hour."

Laci was surprised, because Crystal was usually the first one to shout "peace out" when Laci talked about going home. But perhaps this was a sign that Crystal was really starting to appreciate her company. Most of the time Laci split if the girls were getting ready to go party, but this time she really was tired and was ready to call it a night.

"C'mon, you know that's not true," Laci assured her. "If I didn't want to be around y'all, I wouldn't be. But a chick got to go home and get her beauty rest."

Crystal rolled her eyes and twisted up her lips.

"That's fucked up, Laci," Shaunna said.

"How do you figure that?" Laci asked defensively.

"Forget it." Shaunna waved her off. "Leave, then."

"Yeah, leave if you're going," Monique added.

All of sudden, Crystal surprised Laci yet again. "I don't know about them, but I'm not letting you off so easy this time. I want you to stay, Laci. See, unlike these scared bitches, I ain't afraid to speak my mind. How I see it is that you sit up around us while we drink, smoke, and all that shit, and you even listen to us talk about our *real* sexual experiences. But you don't do none of that. Sometimes it seems like you using us as lab rats. You sit around taking notes on what you don't want to do. It's like you're sitting back and judging us."

Laci's jaw dropped. She couldn't believe that this was how she had been making the girls feel. Finally, this explained why they were so sometimey with her. "You think I've been judging you guys?" Laci asked in disbelief. "Is that how you all feel?" she looked around the room waiting for someone else to speak up.

"Yeah, I guess that sounds about right," Tonette continued. "I mean, how would you feel? While we're passing blunts and bottles, you're on some chill shit. Like you're propped up on a pedestal. You even act like being around weed smoke is gonna kill you."

"But you know I don't do drugs," Laci explained.

"That's some sad shit," Shaunna said. "Weed ain't even a drug. It's a natural herb from the ground, baby—like fuckin' goldenseal or some shit."

"If anything, I would say alcohol is more of a drug than weed," Crystal added. "Who you know smokes a joint, jumps in a car, and takes out a family of five on the expressway?"

"You know?" Shaunna said, giving Crystal some dap.

"I know you don't drink, Laci," Tonette said. "And I can totally dig that. But why you frontin' on the weed? A lil' smoke ain't gon' hurt you."

Laci just stood there silently.

"Tonette, I don't know why you wasting your time," Monique added. "Laci ain't gon' smoke with us. Privileged kids ain't got no time for us around-the-way girls. She's too good. I say let her go get her beauty sleep. The bitch can be pretty and we can be high."

"Y'all gots to chill," said Crystal. "Laci is part of our crew and y'all treating her like an outsider."

Monique and Shaunna looked at each other with confused expressions on their faces. "Since when did you become Laci's best friend?" Monique asked with an attitude.

Crystal gave Monique a *"shut the fuck up"* look. Knowing Crystal so well, Monique knew that look better than anybody. Right then and there she realized she was up to something. The reason for Crystal insisting that Monique call Laci back to make sure that she joined them tonight was starting to come together.

"I ain't saying we're best friends or nothing like that," Crystal responded. "I just don't know why my bitches is tripping over some fucking smoke. I don't believe that Laci thinks she's too good to smoke with us. As a matter of fact, I'll bet that she'll hit the weed just to shut you hatin'-ass bitches up. Ain't that right, Laci?"

"You must be crazy," Shaunna said. "Either that, or you smokin' on some different shit. If she won't hit a little drink, she sure as hell ain't gonna smoke."

The fact that Crystal seemed like she was on her side made Laci feel obligated to at least take one puff. She didn't want to let Crystal down. This was the first time any one of the girls had stood up for Laci.

One pull couldn't hurt. It's just marijuana, Laci thought. *Maybe this will stop the girls from always riding me. If one puff of the magic dragon is all it's going to take to show the girls that I can get down for mines, it's worth it.*

"You got some?" Laci asked Crystal.

"Some what?" Crystal asked.

"Some weed, a joint," Laci said. "I was thinking that I might need a little something to make my rest just that much better."

Laci smiled a mischievous smile and the girls each returned one.

"As a matter of fact, I just happen to have some," Tonette said. "It's in my purse in the living room. Hold on. I'll go get it."

Tonette winked at Crystal and headed into the living room to retrieve the goods.

Shaunna looked at Monique in amazement. They had to admit that Crystal was good. Never in a million years would they have thought that Laci would ever jeopardize her pureness. Sure enough, Crystal was able to sway the naïve girl. Now it was time to sit back and watch the show.

Tonette rejoined the girls in the kitchen with the joint now in her hand. "Tah-dah," she said with a smile. She handed it to Laci, who looked at it as if it were a foreign object. Laci had never actually held a joint, not even to pass it on to one of the other girls when she was sitting in on their puff-puff-pass.

Laci examined the blunt with curiosity.

"What are you waiting for?" Crystal asked, moving the frying pan and turning on the stove burner. "Spark up."

"Why don't one of you guys light it and then pass it to me?" Laci said nervously. The last thing she wanted to do was burn off her bangs trying to light a joint on the stove. "Shaunna, you're good at this—here." Laci stuck the joint in Shaunna's face.

"Now you know I got a Wave Nouveau—if my hair catches on fire we all blowin' up." The girls started cracking up, but Shaunna's face was serious. "You saw what happened to Michael Jackson with that Pepsi commercial."

"Come on, Laci, quit playing with the weed," Monique said, egging her on. "Either light the shit or pass it off. See, Crystal, I told you."

Seeing the smug look on Monique's face made Laci angry. Laci was sick of all of them doubting her and was now more determined than ever to show them that she could hang. Cautiously, she leaned over the flames and lit the blunt.

"That's a girl," Crystal said with a smile. "Now come on in the living room."

The girls followed Crystal into the living room as if they were going to watch a pay-per-view movie. Laci sat down on the couch, and all the girls huddled around to watch her as if she were in a glass box and they had all inserted quarters in a slot to witness her fuck for the first time. Laci looked at the girls looking at her, and then without hesitation, she took two baby pulls.

"Give me a fucking break," Crystal laughed. The other girls stood watching in amazement. They were impressed. They didn't think Laci had the balls. "Did you see those sucker-ass pulls? Look, Laci. That is some good shit and I don't want to see it go to waste. If you gon' do it, do it. Don't be wastin' the shit."

This was the Crystal that Laci was used to, but it was also the Crystal she no longer wanted to doubt her. Laci took two more pulls, only these were deeper. Her throat immediately constricted, causing her to cough. Laci began to feel light-headed.

The girls started laughing. To shut them up, Laci took two more deep pulls, only this time she didn't cough out the smoke; she blew it out. The smell of the weed began to fill her nose. Something was different; it didn't smell like what the girls had smoked before.

Laci looked at Tonette with glassy eyes. Tonette nodded, and like a good little soldier, Laci continued to hit the blunt. Laci could feel her face getting numb and her jaw trying to lock. Her ears began to ring, and she could have sworn she heard "On Cloud Nine" playing in her head. Laci looked at the blunt and smiled. All this time, she had been avoiding something that felt so good. A little toke on the Mary Jane wasn't that bad at all.

"My nigga," Tonette said in amazement. "She did the damn thing. And that's some ol' chronic shit that we ain't never had our hands on before." Tonette winked at Crystal.

Laci smiled as she took another long pull. She had inhaled second-hand smoke from being around the girls when they blazed. She had even caught a buzz from the smoke before, causing her to act a little silly. But she didn't remember ever feeling like this.

"Damn, you blunt hog. We said smoke *with* us," Shaunna said, reaching for the blunt.

"No!" Crystal was quick to say. "Don't smoke that. As a matter of fact, you shouldn't even be around the smoke."

"Bitch, I smoked during every last one of my pregnancies and you know it," Shaunna said. "Keeps me from getting sick."

"No, Shaunna," Tonette insisted. She turned her head and gave her a stern expression. Shaunna threw back a puzzled look. "This one is *especially* for Laci."

"Oh . . ." Shaunna said, nodding her head. A grimace stretched across her lips. "My bad. You right, I shouldn't be smoking anyway."

Shaunna just sat there in the chair, decoding the cryptic language and actions. All of a sudden, the smell of the blunt began to fill the air. Just as Laci had thought, it had a different stench to it. Instantly the girls shot each other looks. Shaunna, realizing what it was, went to the bathroom. Crystal began to shake her head. She was amazed at just how naïve Laci really was. She was almost finished and still didn't realize what she was smoking.

Tonette looked over at Crystal. Crystal cracked a sinister smile. Tonette turned her attention back to Laci and watched her take another puff. She sat there watching Laci get higher than high and didn't do a thing to stop it. She felt like a coward for not telling Laci the real deal at this point, but Crystal was her homegirl. Laci was just another stuck-up bitch, or at least that's what Tonette tried to convince herself.

Laci rolled her head back and looked up at the ceiling. The cracks in the plaster turned into little streams, which Laci tried to follow, but she couldn't stay focused. Her eyes felt like they were going in two different directions at once. She looked at Monique and saw her lips moving, but she could only partially make out what she was saying. All she could see was her teeth, which seemed to be sprouting from her mouth at several odd angles.

She thought it was a side effect of the potent weed and kept pulling on the blunt roach. In her high-ass state, it never occurred to her that none of the other girls put up a fight or even reached for the blunt. Once she was too far gone to comprehend anything, all the girls sat down and had their own private jokes about the hell that they had just introduced Laci to.

CHAPTER 8

On Cloud Nine

LACI AWOKE IN the middle of the night with a headache to end all headaches. Her eyes throbbed as she glared down at her watch. She had been out for at least four hours. *That was some bomb-ass weed,* she thought to herself. *That must be what they mean when they say "chronic."* She tried to stand, but her legs gave out from under her. Laci flopped back down onto the couch and clutched her head in an attempt to stop it from spinning. She searched for something in the room to try and focus on. It was then that she realized she was still at Crystal's. Laci staggered to her feet and proceeded to look around the apartment. She searched the kitchen, both bedrooms, and the bathroom, but there was no sign of the girls. As Laci passed back through the living room, she noticed a note on the coffee table with a joint lying on top of it.

Tried to wake you. Went to the club.
—SBB

Laci sucked her teeth. She really wished that she had been awake, because she was looking forward to partying with the girls for once. A night of dancing and laughing was what she needed to wear her strong-ass buzz off.

Oh well, at least they thought enough of me to leave some more of that chronic, she thought.

Laci put the note down, then picked up the joint. She stared at it for a minute before she started fishing around for a book of matches. She couldn't find any, so she went into the kitchen and turned on the stove. She lit the joint and looked at it.

"Practice makes perfect," she said before taking a hit.

The smoke didn't hit her as hard as the first time. She still gagged, but she was able to hold it in her lungs. The rush from the smoke went directly to Laci's brain, almost making her dizzy. She inhaled the stench from the blunt and realized that this one smelled even less kosher. She could smell the weed, but there was something else that she couldn't quite put her finger on. Laci finished the blunt and tried to figure out what to do next. For some odd reason, she couldn't seem to sit still. She felt alive and wanted to do everything at once. It was as if all the sleep had drained from her body and she had a second wind.

Now, had Laci smoked weed before, certain things would have tipped her off as being not quite right. Weed was a depressant, but Laci felt hyper. Marijuana also had a knack for giving folks the munchies, which Laci didn't have. Actually, she didn't have an appetite at all. The signs would be clear for someone who knew what to look for, but Laci didn't, so she didn't heed the warning going off in the back of her mind.

Laci circled Crystal's apartment three or four times, trying to burn off some of her excessive energy. This went on for a little bit before she started to feel herself coming down off the high.

The girls didn't appear to be coming back anytime soon, so she was on her own for the rest of the night. She put Crystal's door on slam lock and headed into the streets.

"DID YOU SEE that bitch tweekin'?" Shaunna asked, as she sipped her spiked cranberry juice. They had managed to find an old dude outside the store to buy them some alcohol. They decided to head down to the basketball court, where they could scope out the fellas playing a night game of pickup.

"G-i-r-r-l, I thought I was gonna fall out when her jaw locked," Monique laughed, taking a seat on the park bench. "That bitch was s-o-o-o gone. Crystal, did you peep when she started steaming that shit?"

"Huh?" Crystal asked, not really paying attention.

"Earth to Crystal," Monique said, trying to snap her out of her daze. "Damn, you been on some quiet shit since we left the crib. I know you ain't still tripping on how Dink was up on Laci?"

"You peeped that too, huh?" Crystal took a swig of her Pepsi mixed with vodka.

"Who didn't?" Monique said with a snicker.

"Nah, I ain't stunting that bitch," Crystal lied. The truth was, unbeknownst to the girls, she felt terrible about what they had done to Laci. Crystal had an aunt that fell victim to the pipe. She watched her aunt go from a hardworking mother of four to a basehead, sucking dick for her next high.

"Fuck the dumb shit," Monique said. "That lil' bitch deserves a reality check. I'll bet her Mommy would've had a fit had she known her little girl was up in the crib smoking a woo."

Tonette, who hadn't said too much either, decided to jump into the conversation. "Oh, my precious Laci," she said with a horrible British accent. "A crackhead? Well, I never!"

"She's probably gonna feel like shit when she wakes up," Crystal said.

"You don't know the half," Tonette said. "That second one we left her . . . double the lace."

"Girl, you crazy!" Monique shouted hysterically. "You see this crazy bitch, Crystal?"

"What the fuck were you trying to do, kill her?" Shaunna said, shaking her head.

"If she's still buzzing like she was when we left her, she probably wishes she were dead. Ain't that right, Crystal?" Monique laughed.

"Yeah," Crystal chuckled halfheartedly.

Tonette peeped Crystal acting strangely. She knew about her aunt and could see how she probably felt funny, but fuck it. It was too late now. It was a cold world, and fucked-up shit happened every day. "That bitch caught the vapors," laughed Tonette. Monique and Shaunna cracked up. Crystal was still in her own world.

The girls couldn't wait to see Laci so they could find out firsthand what the drugs had done to her. They laughed every time they thought about Laci trying to speak through locked jaws. Finally, Crystal joined in on the snaps. "She sounded like Mushmouth. See how much she talk about her momma and college and shit now. Maybe this is just what Miss Goody-Goody needed to keep that trap closed." Crystal took a puff of her cigarette and laughed—partially because she was amazed at what she'd pulled off and also because she couldn't believe how low she'd stooped.

Though the plan was something Crystal and Tonette had pretty much made happen, all the girls went along with it. But Tonette was their leader. Once she was down, it was a go. Whenever she gave shit the okay, the others just fell in line behind her.

What the crew didn't know was that Tonette harbored a secret—a dark, ugly secret. Everyone just assumed that she didn't like Laci for the same reasons they didn't much care for her, but that wasn't the case.

Tonette actually admired Laci. That was why she pulled her into the crew in the first place. Laci was polite and very pleasant to be around. She was the young lady that none of her dusty friends could ever even fathom becoming. It was this same admiration for Laci that often made Tonette despise her.

Laci came from a nice home and had loving parents. Tonette had been running the streets since she could remember. No one ever gave a shit about her, especially not her drunken-ass mother. Ever since her father had left, all her mother cared about was the bottle and getting a shot of dick here and there. Tonette took to the streets and had a reputation for being one of the toughest female pushers in the South Bronx. Her mother didn't care, as long as she got a check for her twice a month. Unable to find love at home, Tonette found it in the money she was making and finally with Dame, the hustler who'd taken her under his wing and into his home.

Sometimes just looking at Laci or watching her interact with her mother made Tonette want to break down in tears. There were times when she would close her eyes and imagine that Margaret was her mother. She would fantasize about them staying up till all hours of the night having girly talks. Then when she opened her eyes, reality would set in. "Fuck that bitch," Tonette said, downing the rest of her drink.

LACI COULDN'T GET off the train soon enough. The ride from the Bronx to Harlem was a less-than-pleasant one. When she left Crystal's house she was fine, but after being on the train for a few minutes she began to feel sick. Her stomach began to cramp and she became light-headed.

When the train reached 145th Street, she was all too happy to get off. The musty, graffiti-tagged train had done nothing to alleviate her nausea. She jogged up the stairs and was greeted by the brisk night air, music, cars honking their horns, and folks carrying on like it was a nonstop party. Slowly, Laci's head began to clear and she realized that she was starving. She had been at Crystal's all day and hadn't eaten since breakfast. She should have eaten that fried bologna sandwich when she had the chance.

Laci took a detour toward Broadway to grab a bite from the diner. She crossed Amsterdam Avenue and was halfway to Broadway when she had a brilliant idea. *I bet my food would taste better if I smoked another joint.* She made a left and headed back toward St. Nicholas, where she remembered Tonette taking her to a corner store that sold weed in the back. Unsure about which one of the four corner stores at the intersection was the weed spot, Laci slowly walked up to the one with the most dope rides and smooth-looking cats in front. *I know I look stupid. I just hope they don't notice me,* she thought as she tried to figure out how she was going to slip past the circle of guys and into the store.

"Yo, son, you trying to tell me that LL Cool J is better than Rakim? You trippin'," said the guy wearing a green Fila sweat suit. A huge radio was blasting Eric B. & Rakim's "My Melody." The guys, all local hustlers, met up every Saturday night to discuss business, joke, and show off their new cars, clothes, and hoes.

"Damn right, LL is the man. He straight slayed Kool Moe Dee. He's a monster." The other guys stood and watched this heated debate.

"Man, you buggin'. Word is bond, you need to get yo' head

checked and shape up that fucked-up Gumby while you at it." The whole circle erupted in laughter. Laci took this as her only in. As they cracked up, bent over in tears, she sneaked behind them and into the store like a superhero, but with no agenda. She couldn't just walk up to the counter and ask for a nickel bag. Trying to decide what to do, she paced the floor looking for something to purchase. To her surprise, the racks of chips were half empty and what was there was covered with dust. Disgusted with the selection, she walked over to the fridge for a soda. There was hardly anything in the coolers.

I must be in the right store, Laci thought. Figuring she had no other choice, she walked back up to the counter to look in the ice-cream freezer. Nothing was there except some Italian ices, a bag or two of ice, and dead frozen roaches. *Oh my goodness. What am I supposed to do?* With nothing more to lose, Laci contemplated her options: leave the store with nothing and let her high crash or take a chance and ask to buy some weed. *This is what Tonette meant. I need to get courage and stop being a punk.* "Excuse me, sir." The words barely escaped Laci's mouth.

"Laci?" a guy's voice called from the back of the store. Terrified, Laci pretended not to hear him. "Yo, your name is Laci, right?" The guy walked right up behind her and gave the man behind the counter a pound. Laci dared not turn around. He placed his hand on her shoulder and put his face close to hers.

"Dink?" Laci looked out the corner of her eye. "Hi . . . hi, umm . . ."

"Yeah, what you doing down here?"

"Oh, I was in the neighborhood and got thirsty."

Dink didn't believe a word she was saying, but being sort of a nice guy, he thought he'd look out for her. "Laci, this isn't the store you want to be in," he whispered. "Where's Crystal and them?"

"I don't know—they left me and went to the club."

"Really?" *Just my luck*, he thought. "Look, we need to get you out of here. Let me drop you home."

"No, that's fine. I was about to go get something to eat."

"Good, I'm kind of hungry. Let's go, my treat."

No matter how hard she tried, she couldn't get out this. Of course, Dink had a reason to be there. He was handling business in the back. His play cousin, who was a big man in Harlem, had called him down for a meeting. Dink was just coming up the back stairs when he saw a beautiful and familiar face at the counter. He didn't realize it was Laci until he heard her speak; she sounded sweet and innocent, just what had attracted him to her a couple of hours ago. Crazy-ass Crystal was nowhere to be found and since they were miles away from his turf, Dink couldn't help but seize what seemed like a perfect opportunity.

With his hand placed on the small of her back, Dink walked Laci out of the store. When they stepped out front, the group of guys were still jabbering. Suddenly, a car sped up, stopped, and fired four shots into the crowd. Instantly, Dink hovered over Laci, protecting her, and they took off running.

"Come on, my car is up the block!" Dink yelled.

"What . . . what the hell just happened?" Laci was scared to death. If he hadn't pulled her away, she'd probably be standing in the same spot.

"Bring yo' ass, Laci, before you get us shot." The gunmen had successfully hit their target and drove off. The only person left in front of the store was an eighteen-year-old dealer, whose body was riddled with bullets. It was just another Saturday night on the Ave.

Out of breath, they reached Dink's car and got in. Making

sure that Laci wasn't going to go into shock or, worse, throw up all over his tan butter-soft leather interior, Dink started the car and sat there for a few minutes. Laci's mind was all over the place. How had she gone from being a sheltered princess to smoking weed, attempting to buy drugs, and witnessing a murder, all in one day? Her appetite was gone; so was her high. Thinking clearly now, Laci looked at her watch, which read 11:41.

"I have to get home. I have to get home, now." Reality was starting to sink in and tears were beginning to swell up in her eyes.

"Shhh, baby, it's going to be alright. This shit happens all the time. It's a jungle out here, honey, and you shouldn't be here. Let me take you home."

"No," Laci cried.

"Yes. Where do you live?" Dink put the car into drive and pulled out.

"No! I don't want you to take me home."

"Well darling, how are you going to get home then? It's too late for a pretty girl like you to be riding the trains."

"I'll take a cab."

"Fine, let me pay for it." Dink put his hand on her lap.

"I don't need your money!" Laci pulled her leg away. She didn't know what disturbed her more—the shooting, or Crystal's boyfriend getting fresh with her.

Seeing that there was no reasoning with her, Dink got serious. "Okay, I know you don't know me, but trust me, I'm a good guy. I'm just trying to look out for you. What the fuck you were doing down here, I don't know, but I'm not leaving you here. Word to mother."

"Fine. Take me to get a burger and then put me in a cab." Laci didn't want to be left on 145th either. Dink smirked. He'd won the battle.

"I don't know what you're smiling for. I'm paying for my own cab."

"Okay, Ms. Laci. Whatever you want."

CHAPTER 9

Strictly Business

DINK AND HIS partner, Marco, were posted up on the Ave. enjoying the weather. All of the honeys that passed by were checking for the two hustlers. Business was good and everyone knew it.

"Fuck is this lil' nigga at?" Marco complained. "Got a muthafucka standing out here waiting."

Marco was a short fat dude with a flat-top fade with a bleach-blond stripe in the front. His clothes were always fresh and his jewelry game was tight. Marco wasn't the most handsome dude in the hood, so he had to depend on material things like his brand-new Acura Legend, a gigantic mobile phone (that cost $600, $1.39 a minute), and several high-raiser rings with his name spelled out in diamond chips.

"My lil' man will be here," Dink assured him.

"I don't even know why you fuck wit' that lil' nut," Marco said. "Muthafucka is angry all the time. That shit ain't normal."

"Smurf is cool," Dink snickered.

"Cool my ass. That little trigger-happy bastard is dangerous, D. You better keep a leash on that fool."

"I don't need a leash with Smurf. I got a different way of controlling him."

"And what the fuck is that?"

"Books," said Dink, spitting sunflower seed shells on the ground.

"Books?" Marco twisted up his mug.

"Yep. The lil' nigga likes to read. When he's feeling antsy and I ain't got no work for him, I give him a book to occupy his time."

"That lil' muthafucka can read?" Marco asked in disbelief.

"Don't judge a book by its cover," Dink warned. "If you took the time to get to know him, then you'd see he's got some sense."

"That's what *you* say. I say the nigga got issues. What is he reading now?" Marco asked.

"I loaned him *Behold a Pale Horse*."

"Dink," Marco was about to get heated, "I know you ain't give him *my* book?"

Dink sucked his teeth. "Why you always bitchin'? He gon' bring the shit back. Damn!"

"That ain't the point," Marco said, rolling his eyes.

Dink turned and faced him. "Okay then, what *is* the point?"

"The book wasn't yours to give away."

"If the nigga don't bring it back, I'll buy you another one. Matter of fact, how much was it? Never mind. Here." Dink dug down into his pocket and pulled out a roll. He peeled a couple of hundreds off and gave them to Marco. "Buy ten of 'em."

"That ain't the point. You just don't respect people's shit," Marco said, putting the bills in his pocket.

"What you talkin' 'bout? I keep all of my shit tight."

"Yeah, just like you said—*your* shit," Marco pointed out.

"Whateva, yo. Hey, there he go," Dink said, spotting Smurf heading their way. "Yo, Smurf! What up, baby?"

Smurf nonchalantly looked around and assessed everyone in the area. He knew exactly how many people were with Dink and what route would provide the best exit if something popped off. He always paid close attention to his surroundings.

"Ain't nothing," Smurf said, giving him dap. "Another day in the hood."

"What did you think of the book?" Dink asked.

"Yo, that shit is serious," Smurf said, wild-eyed. "The mutha-fuckin' government is grimy."

"That's the world we live in," Marco said. "Now, give me back my book, shorty."

"C'mon, yo. I'm almost finished," Smurf said. "I wanna read the rest of it."

"So you dig it, huh?" Marco asked.

"That shit is dope," Smurf replied.

"Aiight, give it back to me when you finish," Marco said reluctantly.

"Bet." If Smurf had known that the book was Marco's he would have never borrowed it. Codes of the street said he had to respect the dude 'cause he'd been Dink's homeboy since the third grade, but still, Marco was suspect and Smurf didn't want to get too close to him. "What y'all gettin' into?" Smurf asked.

"Why? You wanna roll?"

"Hell yeah," Smurf replied. "I ain't got nothing to do." Dink looked at Marco and nodded.

The three of them walked over to Dink's car. Smurf made it a point to sit right behind Marco. He didn't trust the man, no matter how cool he and Dink were. If Dink gave the word, Smurf would gladly choke the shit out of him.

Marco had been on the scene since before Smurf's time, but Dink had only recently let him into the business. He had no skills when it came down to slanging in the street; however, Dink wanted to make sure his man ate. Smurf respected his boss's call, but he didn't like it. Dink caught the look Smurf was giving Marco in his rearview mirror. Suddenly, he remembered a conversation he and Smurf had a while back.

DINK WAS SITTING in his car, impatiently looking at the clock. He was supposed to meet Marco and Smurf at five o'clock. Smurf was on point, but as usual Marco was late. Over the last couple of weeks, Dink had started to wonder about his boy's strange coming-and-goings. Sometimes Marco would disappear for days at a time, and no one would hear from him. There was no excuse; they both had beepers and car phones. Whenever Dink questioned him about it, on some concern tip, he either had a poor excuse or got defensive. But what could Dink do? Marco was a grown-ass man, served seven years upstate, and had made it clear to Dink that all he wanted to do was grind, make paper, and live large.

"Fuck is this nigga at?" Smurf sounded more annoyed than Dink. "Fat muthafucka always late. This is some bullshit, Dink, you need to check your man."

"Take a chill pill, Smurf. Why you always trippin' when it comes to my peoples?"

"Sorry, cuz." Smurf didn't want to upset Dink, so he changed his tone. "It's just that something ain't right with ya man. I can't put my finger on it, but something is just not right."

"How you figure?"

"It's kinda like when my moms was bringing them niggas

through the crib. I'd look at each one of them and tell what kinda nigga he was—cheat, liar, punk, bully. I could smell it, yo."

"And what do you smell on Marco?" Dink was genuinely interested in Smurf's observations.

"Larceny," Smurf said with a dead serious look in his eyes. "Larceny."

"SMURF," DINK LOOKED at him in the rearview. "This been my main man since like third grade," he said, referring to Marco. "We fight like Cain and Abel sometimes, but this one of the real niggas out here. You know what I'm saying?"

"I hear you." Smurf nodded nonchalantly, looking out of the window.

"Do you?" Dink asked, making sure that if Smurf really did hear him, the shit was loud and clear.

"Yeah, I got you." Smurf caught Dink's stare in the rearview mirror.

"It's hard to find good dudes," Dink said. "You can't trust bitches, no matter what they tell you. Whatever you do, never let a female know your business." Smurf and Marco were silent. "I wonder if bitches will change their style in the 'nineties. New decade, new attitude maybe," Dink said, thinking out loud. "Nah, they ain't gon' be no different . . ." Dink continued talking as if either Smurf or Marco was dying to hear what he had to say.

"What you talkin' 'bout up there, man?" Smurf asked, confused.

"The game," Dink replied. "It makes you cold-blooded to a lot of shit that the average person would get all emotional about. Since you either constantly hustlin' or thinking about ways to hustle, you always think people hustlin' you."

"Huh?" said Smurf.

"I'll give you an example," Dink said, clearing his throat. "Sometimes when I hear someone say somethin' that don't make sense, my antennas go up and I starting thinkin' they tryin' to swindle me. That doesn't mean that they are. It's just that all the shifty shit you do makes you defensive like that. You have to be careful. You can ruin a lot of relationships with that bullshit. I'm still battling with that. It ain't easy."

"He right, Smurf," Marco added, finishing off the Devil Dog he was eating. "Niggas'll try to glaze you all of the time, but you have to be sophisticated enough to be able to differentiate between the straight shooter and the one tryin' to take you. You have to work on that balance."

"Balance?" Smurf questioned.

"Yeah," Dink said. "Niggas mistake kindness for weakness, so you have to be cool breeze but yet rule with an iron fist. You got to know when to go hard and when to finesse shit."

Smurf absorbed every word. He knew how to be silent and let the teachers teach. This was by far his biggest asset.

"I can tell by what you just said that you's a smart nigga," Marco said, turning down the car radio.

"Smart? I ain't said nothing," Smurf protested.

"That's the point," said Dink. "Most niggas know too much and can't take direction. They always tryin' to get you to believe how true they are. You just listen and sop it up like a mop." Smurf had no comment. "That's why I gave you that piece back in the day. I don't just give niggas I don't know shit, especially without seeing any dough. In you, I saw loyalty and someone truly willing to do whatever it takes to rise above the dumb shit. That's why I put you down. You still got a long education ahead of you, but you're a good student. I wish my nigga Earl was here to meet you."

"What happened to him?" Smurf inquired.

"Oh, he ain't dead or nothing like that. He doin' life right now," Dink said sorrowfully.

"Life?" Smurf said with a deep sigh, lowering his head. "Shit, nigga might as well be dead. What did he do, anyway?"

Marco and Dink looked at each other.

"What you've been doing for the past two years," Dink said. "You came along not long after he got knocked. Earl was thorough, too. You got big shoes to fill, kid."

"Sounds like this conversation is long overdue," Smurf said.

"Well, then I guess it's better late than never," Dink said. "But listen up. You've got an edge over Earl, and that's your age and size. People don't even think you're old enough to piss straight, let alone drop a nigga. Even though you 'bout to be eighteen, you look like a baby. That's why they never see it coming. Police wouldn't even give you a second look. And if you do get bagged, it's a slap on the wrist. You won't even have a record."

Marco turned the air conditioner up to max, and a frigid wind swept through the car. Dink looked at him like he was crazy. The weather was warm, but it wasn't burning up. Summer hadn't even begun.

"Marco, turn that shit down," Dink ordered.

"Damn, it's hot in here," Marco complained as he turned the air down. There were three things that you could count on Marco to be—hungry, hot, and out of breath.

"You know it's hot in this bitch," he continued. "If you open the glove compartment, you'll see the devil in there sittin' on an ice cube."

"Crazy muthafucka," Dink said with a slight laugh.

"Say, let me ask you something," Smurf said. "I've been down with y'all niggas for a minute, right?"

"Your point?" Dink asked.

"My point is, when am I gonna get to meet the rest of the crew?" Smurf said, leaning forward to the point where his head was almost perfectly positioned between Marco's and Dink's. "So far I've only met a couple of cats."

"Yeah, and you don't need to know the rest," Marco added. "You're the best-kept secret, so to speak. The less niggas you know, the less they know you, the better off you'll be."

"That's right," Dink cosigned. "They're gonna know who you are, but they ain't gotta know what you do. That's my business. Plus, those low-level, bottom-of-the-totem-pole niggas get replaced a lot. Never can tell who's gonna make it and who ain't."

"What about that cat Dame I've been hearing so much about?" Smurf asked.

Dink and Marco exchanged glances.

"You'll meet him soon enough," they answered in unison.

RICK YOUNG, A.K.A. Dame, was well known for outsmarting the police a couple of years earlier. They thought they had him, but he had mastered a trick that some of the young hustlers weren't up on yet. When the police searched him, the drugs were nowhere on his person. Frustrated, they had to let him go. They couldn't figure out what the hell he did with the drugs. He had stuffed them in his ass. It was a trick he had learned from his brother while he was up North.

As a boy, Rick was made fun of by his peers. He was called ugly and females paid him no attention. His family ignored him, and his teachers neglected his needs in the classroom. If that wasn't enough, he was a fat boy except he didn't beat box. With a bad acne problem and breasts, he was nicknamed *Titty Ricky*. Needless to say, many fights were started over this.

Rick's self-esteem took a beating during his adolescent years with no father to turn to. He became violent, and his aggression was mostly directed toward women. Tyrone, Rick's father, was an average-looking country Negro with no talent. Rick had only seen him twice. He favored his mother, though, and blamed her for what he was told was his repulsive appearance. He despised her, and any female that reminded him of her, for his pain.

By the time he reached his late teens, peddling drugs had made Rick's confidence soar. He was the man when he was on the grind. For the first time in his life he had the attention of females, and he treated them all like shit. Anytime a female pushed his buttons, he'd take his deep-rooted personal frustrations out on her. And it wasn't just Rick's outward appearance that caused him so much pain. It was the fact that he secretly craved the love from a woman that he never got as a child.

Rick also had a reputation as being somewhat extra. He had been doing his own thing out in Brooklyn before joining forces with Dink. He was a good earner and brought a multitude of things to the team. Most notable was his lust for violence. He was a hothead, who believed in doing things only one way—his way. He and Dink constantly butted heads, but the money they made together overshadowed all the bullshit.

"Yo, speaking of Dame, that nigga tryin' to run whores now, on the sneak tip. Muthafucka always doing some side shit. Yo, we need to check him, Dink," said Marco.

Marco had never liked Dame because Dame had a file on him. He wasn't sure of the exact contents of the file, but Dame was always giving him a look like, "*I got yo' ass, nigga.*"

CHAPTER 10

Triple-Crossed

IT HAD BEEN four days since Laci had seen her girls. None of them wanted to be the one to make initial contact with her. They chose to sit back and allow Laci to get at them so that they could see where her head was. Laci could have cared less about who made contact first. She had spent the past ninety-six hours fantasizing about getting high, desperately wanting that feeling back.

By day two, Laci had started to feel under the weather. At one point, her mother had walked into her bedroom and found her keeled over. They both thought that Laci might have been coming down with the flu, so she stayed home from school Monday and Tuesday.

Laci tried to stay in bed during that time, but she grew restless as the hours passed. For some reason she couldn't stop thinking about getting high. She longed for that same high she felt from her first hit. But she feared that it would never be like the first time. And although the shit had stunk to high hell, it took her to paradise. She shivered just remembering the feeling.

Margaret tried to make small talk with her, but Laci only half-listened and hardly responded. All she could think about was getting high. Her mother went on and on about graduation and Puerto Rico. Laci wasn't trying to hear anything, not unless the principal was going to hand her a joint instead of a diploma, or her mother was sending her off to Puerto Rico with a suitcase full of weed. Fuck clothes. She would lie around butt-naked blazin'.

Laci was damn near ready to climb the walls that seemed to be closing in on her. The high was calling her, and she couldn't resist. She thought it was cool. Now she had a weed habit, just like the girls. Laci had no idea what tune the devil was about to play for her on his fiddle. She didn't care, either. She was just happy to be dancing. Now she knew why the girls hardly made a move without getting high. She sort of missed them, or maybe it was the weed she knew they could get for her. Either way, she knew that she was missing something. Laci decided to give Tonette a call. Maybe Tonette could help her fill the void. Laci picked up the phone and dialed the number.

"Who dis?" Tonette answered on the second ring with a stink attitude.

"Hey, it's Laci," she said sheepishly. "What you doing?" She spoke as if nothing was up, and Tonette did the same.

"Nothing. I'm waiting for Shaunna's pregnant ass," Tonette said. "Where you been hidin'?" Tonette patiently waited for Laci's response. If Laci was going to beef, this was going to open the door for her to do so.

"I've been a little sick," Laci told her.

"Really?" Tonette sighed with relief. "Everything cool?"

"Yeah, probably just getting a cold." Laci sniffed.

"Say, how did you like that weed?" Tonette asked, again opening up the door of opportunity.

"It was dope," Laci said excitedly. "I was actually gonna ask if you had any more." There was a pause. "Well, do you?"

Tonette's mouth dropped. "Listen to little Miss Pothead," she said with a cunning smile. "Sorry, girl. The last of that got smoked up."

"Damn," Laci said, sounding defeated.

"I know where to get more," Tonette said teasingly. "But it's a little expensive." *Fuck it,* she thought. The shit must not have fazed her like they thought it would. It didn't kill her either, so everything was all-good. Anything this bitch did now, she was doing on her own.

"How much?" Laci asked, looking at her purse, which was sitting on the dresser.

"Depends. Usually you've gotta buy it in bulk, but for about a hundred I can probably do something for you."

"I don't know if I've got that much on me," Laci said, thumbing through her cash. All she had left was five dollars after paying for her cab ride home the other night.

"Don't sweat it," Tonette said nonchalantly. "We can get some regular green."

Laci needed to get exactly what she'd had the other night. Anything less just wouldn't cut it. "No, I want that chronic you gave me before. Give me a little while to try and scrape up that hundred."

"Okay. Meet me at the 4 train on 161st Street around four o'clock," Tonette instructed. She hung up before Laci could answer. There was no need to wait. She knew Laci would be there.

• • •

MINUTES AFTER TONETTE got off the phone with Laci, Shaunna showed up at her doorstep. She wobbled into the house and flopped down on Tonette's couch. Shaunna's partying, drinking, and smoking was starting to catch up with her. Trying to live the life and carry a child was hard work.

"Girl, you're just in time," Tonette said.

"In time for what?" Shaunna asked.

"To see some funny shit," Tonette giggled. "I just hung up the phone with you-know-who."

"Who?" Shaunna said.

"Who you think, yo?" Tonette said, sucking her teeth and placing her hand on her hip.

"Word?" Shaunna said, leaning forward. "Did you call her? What did she say? Did she cuss you out?"

"Listen to this," Tonette said, sitting down next to Shaunna. "We're about to take her over to 161st to get some rock."

"No way," Shaunna said in complete disbelief. "You need to cut it out. Don't you think once is enough? You're gonna give the girl a fucking habit. You seen what happened to Quita."

"Fuck Quita. She did that without our help."

"Whatever, you never liked her either. Especially after you found out about her and Dame."

Tonette was fuming; she'd never mentioned Quita since their falling-out. Quita had been a major part of the South Bronx Bitches, but they kicked her out two weeks after Laci came into the picture. "This Laci shit ain't on me," Tonette protested. "That ho called and asked me to get it for her."

Shaunna shook her head in disagreement. "Tonette, I think you're going a lil' too far with this shit. I mean, ha ha, joke's over. We all had a good laugh. The bitch passed initiation or whatever you want to call it. It's over."

"Damn, you starting to sound like Crystal," Tonette said defensively. "I called her to let her in on what was going down, and she tried to dead me, too. Fuck is everybody so worried about Laci for? I didn't see anybody taking that woo from her the other night."

"Whatever," Shaunna said.

"Yeah, whatever," Tonette said, waving her off as she got up from the couch. "Just bring yo' ass on so we don't miss her when she shows up."

Reluctantly, Shaunna pulled herself up off the couch and followed the leader.

BY THE TIME Tonette and Shaunna got to the train station, Laci was already waiting. She still looked like her normal stuck-up self. Her hair was slicked back in a big, curly ponytail and she was wearing a pair of creased Calvin Klein blue jeans with a crisp white shirt. She might have looked like the same Laci on the outside, but Tonette could tell by the way she was acting so antsy and dancing in place that something totally different was going on with her.

"What up, girl?" Tonette asked with a fake sisterly grin.

"Hey, girl," Laci said, hugging her. "What up, Shaunna?"

"Hey," Shaunna said flatly.

Laci peeped Shaunna's bland-ass greeting and made a mental note of it. Every time she came around, one of them found a reason to have an attitude. It never failed. She was so happy to see Tonette that she didn't even care. Let Shaunna have her attitude. All Laci was thinking about was chilling and getting her smoke on.

"So, where to?" Laci asked, getting right to the matter of the meeting.

"Right to the point, huh?" Shaunna mumbled.

"Shut up," Tonette warned her. "It's only a few blocks from here. Come on, y'all."

Tonette led the way. The girls cut into a block that was filled with short tenement buildings. Some were leaning and some had just fallen completely down. People moved up and down the block, trying to hustle this or that. Tonette waved them off and headed directly for the man she was looking for.

Marvin was an older man who looked like he had seen better days. He sat on the hood of someone's car, rapping to a cracked-out-looking chick. Tonette made eye contact with him and beckoned him over. "Gimme your money, Laci," she said, extending her hand. Laci placed five twenties in her palm. "Hold up, y'all," Tonette said, excusing herself from the two of them. She walked over to Marvin and started speaking.

Laci looked around the neighborhood, scared to death. She was afraid that someone might spot her and tell her mother. But no one that her mother knew would be caught dead in this part of town. Although Laci hung out with her girls in the hood, she never really chilled hard in some of the shadier parts of town. Being in such proximity to so many addicts made her uneasy.

Shaunna peeped how noided Laci was acting. She just shook her head. It was obvious what she was becoming.

"Let's go, y'all," Tonette said, walking past her friends.

"Did you get it?" Laci asked hopefully.

"Just bring yo' ass," Tonette said, continuing her stroll.

Laci scrambled behind her like a lost puppy. Tonette got a kick out of stringing her along. It made her feel good to be on top for once. Laci had tasted the drug for only a short time, and she was already jonesin'.

"Let's hop in a cab," Laci said, looking around. "I wanna get up outta here."

"What's the matter?" Shaunna teased. "Ain't got no stomach for the hood?"

"No, I just wanted to get off this block," Laci lied. Between all the activity and Laci's urge to get high, she felt like she was going to go bananas. When the gypsy cab pulled up, Laci was the first one to hop in it.

Tonette was slick with her shit. When they got in the cab, Laci asked to see what her hundred dollars had bought her. Tonette fed her a bullshit excuse about the area being too hot to pull it out right then. During the ride, Shaunna engaged Laci in conversation while Tonette discreetly rolled the woo. By the time they had reached their destination, Laci was presented with two freshly rolled joints.

SUNSET IN THE hood meant the streets came alive. Tonette and her crew had been in the same spot for the last couple of hours. Laci sat on the bench higher than high. She was looking off into space and having trouble feeling her tongue. This was the kind of high she had been craving.

By this time, Monique and Crystal had joined them. When Monique had first walked up on the girls, she immediately knew what time it was. She had seen Laci wear that glazed-over look at Crystal's house. She looked at the stupid-ass grin Laci was wearing and had to turn her head to keep from laughing in her face. She understood the first time, but how in the hell did they get Laci to smoke for a second time without her figuring out that something was up?

Laci, being the kind-hearted fool that she was, offered to let

Tonette spark one. Tonette told her that she was trying to go for a city job over the summer and didn't want to piss dirty. Shaunna used the pregnant excuse again, so smoking was out of the question for her. The couple of times that she passed the blunt to Crystal, she was too busy talking and carrying on to realize that Crystal never once hit it and only held it between her fingers. Just like the first time, Laci was on her own.

The more Laci smoked, the more she fell in love with the drug. Tonette had put more crack in the blunt than weed, but Laci wouldn't have noticed. All she cared about was sucking in the death mist that had become the object of her affection. Laci had been officially introduced to her monkey.

The girls pretty much just sat around watching Laci make a fool of herself. The crack had her bugging. First she kept pacing back and forth, talking about how much energy she had. Then the fool started singing The Temptations' "Cloud Nine" at the top of her lungs. *"I'm doing fine... up here on Cloud Nine... I'm gonna sail up higher... up, up and away..."* Shaunna felt like she was going to go into premature labor tripping off of Laci's antics.

"Yo," Laci said, hopping up for at least the fifth time, "I'm mad hyped. Any other time y'all would be trying to talk me into sneaking into a club or something. But now everybody just wants to sit around and look at each other. We need to do something, anything. Let's just make a move."

"Why don't you just chill," Crystal said. She had had enough of Laci. She wished she had just kept her ass at home.

"Fuck that." Laci snapped her fingers, continuing to hum the song. "We need to be in the streets, y'all. Why are we wasting the night?"

"Listen to Action Jackson over here," Monique said, sucking

her teeth. "You been watching too much BET. Why don't you sit yo' high ass down?"

Laci paused for a moment, getting ready to follow Monique's orders like she normally would have done, just to keep things down. But a voice inside her told her to rebel. "You know what?" Laci said, putting her hands on her hips. "Fuck you!" Everyone's jaw dropped. "Every time you come around you bring your bullshit with you. Take that shit home with your tired ass."

This was the first time they had ever heard Laci come out of her face. Crack or no crack, Monique was not going to tolerate Laci's mess.

"Fuck you say to me?" Monique got to her feet.

"You heard me," Laci said defiantly. "You stay coming at me with beef. You need to check yaself, bitch."

"Ain't this a bitch?" Monique said in disbelief. "This ho been sittin' back taking notes. Well, write this down." Monique lunged at Laci and grabbed her by her shirt. Laci was caught totally off guard. Monique snuffed her square in the jaw. Laci tried to defend herself, but Monique was a street fighter, while she had never been in a fight. Once they saw blood, Tonette broke it up.

"Cool the fuck out!" Tonette shouted at Monique.

"Fuck that," Monique barked. "I'm tired of this bitch. You ain't shit, Laci."

"Fuck you," Laci said, patting her lip. "You got some nerve. Low-life bitch, you're just a bitter."

"Low-life? I got ya low-life, you fucking crackhead."

The other girls started to become uneasy. Monique's anger was making her careless with the secret.

"Bitch, you wish. I could never fuck wit' that shit. I got too much smarts, unlike your dumb ass. And weed ain't hard core. Y'all said yourself that it's a natural herb."

"You so green that it's fucking pitiful," Monique chuckled. "You think you so muthafuckin' street, but you ain't nothing but a prissy bitch. A street bitch would know the difference between crack and weed, dummy."

At that moment, you could have heard a pin drop. The leaves on the trees rustled while a basketball bounced unattended somewhere in the distance. Monique's statement froze the whole crew. Laci looked over at the girls. Shaunna had her head down and was rubbing her belly, and Tonette was looking away.

Laci closed her eyes and took a couple of deep breaths. "Wh . . . what?" she stuttered. No one had an answer for her. Tonette shot a murderous stare at Monique, letting her know that she would answer for her dumb-ass move. Shaunna shook her head, and Crystal just turned away. Things were falling apart fast.

"All y'all do is fuckin' run y'all's mouth," Laci said with a mixture of fury and fear. "Now you mean to tell me that not one of you bitches has shit to say?"

Laci ran her hands across her eyes and over the crown of her head. Her brain was hurting. She began to pace and panic. "Oh, my God. Oh, my God," she repeated.

"Mo is tripping, girl," Tonette said. "Why the fuck would we give you crack? We're your fam."

"Y'all my family, huh? My fuckin' fam?" Laci asked, teary-eyed. "Fam doesn't try to hurt each other, not like the way y'all did me. All I've ever wanted to do was to fit in. The way y'all have each other's back—the unspoken love y'all have for one another . . . that's all I've ever wanted to be a part of. I've allowed y'all to do damn near everything but shit on me. Y'all talk about me like a dog in my face. I can only imagine what y'all say about me when I'm not around. Fam?" Laci shook her head as tears poured down her face. "Fam doesn't try to condemn one another for wanting to be something in life more than just somebody's baby's mama or somebody's bitch. Fuck kinda fam is this?" Laci ran off.

Tonette sat silently for a moment. "Fuck this. I can't let the shit go down like this," she said, blinking the moisture out of her eyes. But it was too late. Laci was out of sight.

CHAPTER 11

Callin' Shots

"WHO THE FUCK is this Titus nigga?"

As the summer of '89 neared, Dink had gathered his executive branch together to discuss how they were going to rid themselves of an infringing competitor. "All I keep hearing is Titus this and Titus that. Somebody tell me *something.*" Dink was raving mad at this point. It took a lot to get him angry these days, but some shit got under his skin like tattoos. "Y'all niggas is out there, right?" Dink continued. "Fuck is going on? Everywhere I turn a nigga is telling me Titus stories, but my boys don't know shit? Fuck is up?" Dink slid down the window of his Saab 900 Turbo to let in some air. The four bodies in the car were generating heat.

"Yo, I'm like you," Marco responded. "I don't know who the fuck he is. But what I do know is that he's on one of our blocks gettin' money. At least that's the word on the street."

Dame didn't see Titus as the threat everyone else in the car did. He figured that since it was his block the dude was violating, he should be the one stressing. Dame would handle things like he always did—his way. Cracking a chipped-tooth smile, Dame began to speak. "I think y'all overreacting. It ain't even that serious," he said nonchalantly.

Dink looked at Dame as if he had lost his mind. Dame had a bad habit of testing Dink, and now was definitely not the time.

Dink took out his burner and placed it on the armrest between Marco and himself. "Repeat that." Dink turned to face Dame in the backseat. "I want to make sure I heard you right."

Dame loved a challenge and feared no one. He countered Dink's attempt to intimidate him by pulling out his own piece, cocking it, and resting it on his lap. "I said it ain't that serious," he replied in a daring tone.

"How the fuck you figure?" Marco spat.

All eyes were focused on Dame.

"Because," he continued, "I seen that nigga around and he ain't moving nothing major. He small and can be taken out in a second. I ain't sweatin' that fool."

"Then why you ain't say that shit when I asked?" Dink said.

"And where you seen him at?" Smurf added.

Dame had no respect for the seventeen-year-old gunman and resented the fact that Smurf felt like he was in a position to ask him anything. The lil' nigga was a nobody to him and didn't deserve to be answered.

"Where?" Dink said.

"Washington Avenue," Dame said. "Around my way."

"Okay, so this is your problem?" Dink said, scratching his chin. "How long has this nigga, Titus, been violating'?"

"Only a couple of months," Dame said, picking his nails.

Dame's nonchalant demeanor angered Dink. "Two months?" Dink barked. "You got muthafuckas disrespectin' the hustle for months and you ain't say nothing? Other cats lookin' at that like our team ain't keepin' it funky. Soon one of them smaller crews is gonna try to climb up the food chain."

"Look, man," Dame said, clapping his hands together. "If I felt the nigga needed to be seen, then it would've been done already. That's my spot. I know what I'm doing, kid. If his hand call for it, then he goes. When I off the muthafucka, niggas gon' know what the truth is. Right or wrong? Right now he comfortable thinkin' he movin' in, but he can always be touched. I got it covered."

"Dame, I understand that you do shit different," Dink said, "but we countin' on you to keep it tight where you at. Forget about Titus for now. What's the deal with these bitches you fuckin' with? They runnin' their mouths, and niggas tellin' me shit they ain't supposed to know."

Two years isn't much time in the game, but Smurf already knew what Dame represented. He was a cancer to their crew. Big-headed niggas like him were always the downfall of the great dynasties. His gut told him that he would be called on to put Dame to sleep sooner or later.

"Believe me, I got this," Dame assured Dink. "I'm gonna take care of the big-mouth bitch and some mo' shit in a hot one. I know just what bitch you talkin' 'bout, too. Fucking dumb bitch. I told her to play her cards right and she would be good, but a fucking bitch is always gonna be a bitch. I was actually kinda digging her, too."

"That's why I always tell y'all to leave them hoes alone," Dink said. "Dame, you're either gonna hustle or pimp. You can't swing both, 'cause it's fucking up our action." No sooner than Dink had finished his sentence, two of Dame's girls walked up to Dink's parked car.

"What up, daddy?" Julie said. "No wonder I ain't seen you. You spending all your time with these cats." Julie was one of

Dame's best pieces of ass and she got away with just as much as his main girl, Quita.

"Go wait in my car," Dame said to her flatly.

"Hey, Dame," Naomi said, licking her lips. She usually stayed quiet, but the sight of Marco had her talkative. "Your friend lookin' for a date?"

"Yo, Dame," Marco said. "Get your bitch before you be pickin' her up off the floor."

Dame smiled. "Talk to her, nigga. It ain't gon' cost you nothin'."

"Yeah, what you afraid of?" Naomi asked. "Don't tell me that you scared of little ol' me, big man," she crooned in her white thigh-high boots and skin-tight tube dress that was so short her pussy hairs were damn near showing.

"Shoot, scared of what?" Marco said, shooing her away. "Get the fuck out of here. I'll blow your little back out."

Smurf sat in the backseat confused, watching Marco turn down what he thought was a nice piece of tail—and free at that. "Sh-e-e-e-i-t. If that was me, I'd know what to do," Smurf said. "She wouldn't have to say that shit twice."

Dame began to chuckle. "Yo, even lil' man back here ready to do the do," he said. "You supposed to lead the younger niggas by example. You ain't showing him shit, Marco."

"C'mon, big boy," Naomi begged. "Take me somewhere. I like you." Naomi ran her hand alongside Marco's cheek. "I'm clean, and I know this pussy is good. C'mon, baby. I ain't had no good dick in a while. Show me somethin'."

"Ooh-wee," Smurf said and let out a whistle. "If he don't want none, hook me up. Hey, girl, I'll take care of you," he said to Naomi.

"You cute, too," Naomi said, winking at him. "But you a little young, sweetie. Come back in a couple of years when you grow some hair on that chin of yours."

"What? You crazy," Smurf said, offended. "I know what to do. I wouldn't be sittin' there stupid. I'd be all up in that ass."

"Smurf, you want a taste?" Dame asked.

"Hell yeah."

This was one of those rare moments when Dame's heart went soft. "Hey, girl," he said to Naomi. "Leave that fat nigga alone and give my boy Smurf here a shot of somethin'. Dink, we done here?"

"Yeah, we finished for now, but do me a favor and get these bitches the fuck off the block."

"Naomi . . . Julie," Dame called out the window, "go sit in my car." Dame threw Naomi the keys. "Smurf, it's on you. Go with them to the car. I'll be there in a second."

Before Dame got out of the car, Dink made sure he understood how serious the situation was. "Yo, I don't want to have to hear about this nigga Titus no more, man," Dink said. "I'm trustin' that you gon' take care of business. If you can't handle it, let me know and I'll replace you with someone who can."

"What did I say?" Dame frowned. "I told you I got it. I'm gon' take care of the nigga. You startin' to doubt me, yo?"

"And them girls?"

Dame sighed out of frustration. "You don't even have to say it. I got it. You got my word on that. My word is bond." Dame got out of the car and joined Smurf and the girls. Marco and Dink glared at him as he walked away.

Dink spoke to Dame as if he were still within earshot. "It ain't the fact that I'm starting to doubt your word. I'm just wondering if I should have ever given your word any weight in the first place."

"I guess we'll find out soon enough," Marco said.

CHAPTER 12

Me, Myself, and I

LACI WALKED THROUGH the streets aimlessly, trying to stop the tears from falling. All she wanted was for the girls to accept her, and she'd ended up playing the fool. But she couldn't fully believe Monique's accusations. A falling-out is a falling-out, but to slip her crack? Her brain couldn't and wouldn't process it. Finding that shit out seemed almost equivalent to finding out that she had AIDS. Either way, she felt like her life would be over.

She continued to wander the streets until a thought entered her mind. She needed a joint to calm her nerves. Yeah, after a joint she could relax and all of the dumb shit would go away. Laci thought about the numbing effect of the drug and began to shiver.

What the hell was she thinking about? No matter what she was doing, the thought of getting high would come to mind. Yesterday, she had gone to the supermarket and her mother asked her to hand her a bunch of spinach. Laci stood there wondering what would happen if she dried out the spinach leaves and smoked them. From what the girls told her, weed was a plant, and so was spinach. It couldn't be that much different. All this made her further suspicious of Monique's accusations.

Laci tried to tell herself over and over again that her peoples wouldn't go out like that. In all actuality, if Tonette wanted to slip her something, she had every opportunity. Laci never watched her roll; she trusted Tonette, so there was no need. But the more she thought about it, the more possibilities came into play. Maybe she was just being paranoid. She'd read somewhere that weed did that to you. Realizing that she was shivering. Laci thought maybe she needed some smoke to calm her nerves.

Laci caught herself in mid-thought. There she was thinking about getting high again. For some reason, she couldn't seem to focus on anything else. She wasn't a seasoned smoker like the rest of the girls, but she had smoked enough weed over the last few days to notice the difference in the highs. When Tonette had first set her out, Laci felt like she was on top of the world. It was the best feeling she'd ever had. She'd tried to reach that special place time and time again, only to fall short. She couldn't seem to get that blast that she had the first time, but she was determined to keep smoking until she did.

Before Laci had even realized it, she was back on the block Tonette had taken her to when they got the weed earlier. She didn't know exactly where she was, but she recognized Marvin. Suddenly Laci had a thought: *Maybe Marvin would score some weed for me.* With getting high on the brain, she didn't hesitate to approach him.

"Hey," she called over to him.

"Who that?" Marvin asked through slit eyes.

"I came over here earlier with, Tonette. Remember?"

"Oh," Marvin said, scratching his chin. "What's up, redbone?"

"Chillin'. I wondered if you could do me a favor," she said.

"What ya need, Miss?"

"The same thing you got for Tonette earlier."

"So that was for you?" he asked, surprised.

"Yeah," she said, looking at the ground. "I don't smoke all the time, just when I need to relax."

"Sure, kid," Marvin said. "Okay, let me get your bread."

"This is all I got," Laci said, handing him forty dollars. "Can I get something with this?"

"Yeah," he said, stuffing the bills in his pocket. "Gimme a minute." He then walked up the block and whispered something to one of the kids who were standing on the corner. A few minutes later, he came back to where Laci was waiting. "Come on," he said, motioning for her to follow him. Marvin led Laci around the corner and handed her four cellophane bags with rocks in them.

"What's this?" Laci asked, looking at the bags. "I didn't ask for this. I asked for what Tonette got earlier."

"What you think I just gave you? That's what Tonette copped when she came through earlier."

Laci felt as if she went blind and deaf at the same time. She couldn't believe what Marvin was telling her. It was just like Monique had said. Laci had been smoking laced weed. She felt like screaming, but the onlooking addicts put her on pause. Laci walked away from Marvin without saying a word. All she could do was look at the crack and cry.

LACI RODE THE train home but didn't feel like going home yet. Instead, she hopped back on the train—this time headed downtown—and went to The Village. She walked up and down the side streets. She didn't have a destination, but she felt the need to keep moving.

She found a little store off to the side and ducked in to get a few things. Laci picked up a can of Tab and a pack of gum. When she got to the counter, she asked for a pack of Newports and a lighter. Laci never smoked, but she was stressed and willing to try something else new.

As Laci scanned the racks behind the counter, she noticed a variety of little corn pipes. She asked the clerk if she could take a closer look at one. She had seen Crystal smoke weed out of pipes before and had always been curious. She added the pipe to her purchase.

Following the flow of people traffic, Laci found herself by the Westside Pier, the nonstop party spot of New York's gay kids, drag queens, druggies, and misfits. She took a seat on an empty bench. She pulled a cigarette from her pack and placed it between her lips. She flicked the lighter and the flame stood at attention. The orange serpent swayed back and forth, waiting for its mistress to command it. Laci slowly placed the light to the cigarette and inhaled. She gagged from the horrid tobacco taste and spat on the ground. Laci tossed the cigarette and scratched it from her new bad-habit list.

There went her only method of calming her nerves. Just then, Laci pulled out the bag of rocks. She held one of the tiny stones between her thumb and index finger and twirled it. She couldn't believe how something so small could reshape a person's life. Round and round she turned it, becoming more fascinated as it spun.

I'm doing fine... up here on Cloud Nine... I'm gonna sail up higher... up, up and away...

Laci couldn't believe her girls would have been grimy enough to slip her crack. Had it been more than weed in the blunt, wouldn't she have noticed it? Shouldn't she have noticed it? There were countless possibilities running through her head, but she couldn't be sure which one was accurate.

"Crackhead," she mumbled. "Yeah, right." Laci knew there was no way that Tonette could have slipped her crack without her noticing. It was laughable at best. Laci decided to get rid of the rock and be done with it.

Laci tossed the rock to the ground and shook the rest of the stones onto the seat next her. For lack of anything better to do, she decided to burn them. She took her lighter and placed the flame on the rocks. Entranced, Laci watched the stones fizzle and pop, producing a foggy yellow smoke. Laci smiled at the melting pile, until she caught a whiff. Her body froze in place.

At first the stench burned her nose, but then it became strangely familiar. She started to bug because she knew that her nose wasn't lying to her. She leaned in closer to get a better smell and sure enough, it was the same smell that she had encountered at Crystal's house. This was her weed.

I'm doing fine... up here on Cloud Nine... I'm gonna sail up higher... up, up and away...

Me, a crackhead? How? Her brain just couldn't seem to process the thought. She had seen crackheads in the streets, but she didn't fit the profile. Crackheads were degenerates who came from broken homes. No, she didn't fit the profile at all.

Laci was brought out of her daze by a warm, sticky sensation against her fingers. She looked down and noticed that some of the melting crack had gotten on her hands. She looked at the gooey substance and observed it. There was something beautiful about it—something that wouldn't allow her to look away.

The smell of it put her in a tranquil state. Her mouth began to water and her hand moved involuntarily. Without even realizing it, Laci had the corn pipe in her hand. She looked from the pipe to the goo as if she were figuring out some great math equation.

"I need to know," she said, teary-eyed. Laci packed some of the goo into the pipe and stared at it. Her hand shook uncontrollably as she raised the pipe to her lips. She couldn't believe what she was about to do. Her poor mother's heart would break if she could see her right now. Laci put the flame to the pipe and took a hesitant pull. The smoke rushed to her brain, and there was no doubt in her mind this time . . . *I'm doing fine on Cloud Nine . . . I'm riding high on Cloud Nine . . .*

CHAPTER 13

The Hit

YOU SHOULD'VE SEEN my nigga," Dink said, passing the joint to Marco. "Lil' nigga came running around the corner talkin' 'bout, 'Floor this bitch.' This nigga was on some real *Untouchables*-type shit." He leaned up against his car and nodded his head as if he were a proud poppa.

"So this lil' nigga got down, huh? Titus had it coming though." Marco took a pull. "Niggas on the streets better know to steer clear of young Smurf."

Smurf sucked his teeth. "Come on, son. Don't be puttin' my business out there like that. I like to stay on the low."

"Ain't nobody gonna blow ya spot," Dink assured him.

"I wasn't talking about you," Smurf said, cutting his eyes at Marco.

Marco caught the look that Smurf was giving him and wasn't comfortable with it. The lil' nigga was giving him the same look that Dame had given him. He wondered if the two of them had discussed anything when Smurf smashed Dame's ho.

Dink saw the look that Smurf was giving Marco and wondered what the deal was. Ever since Dink started having Marco around full-time, Smurf had been looking at him sideways. For some reason, Smurf just wasn't feeling him. This was something Dink would have to think on.

Before he could ponder it further, Dame came walking around the corner. Dink could tell that he had something on his mind because his nostrils were flaring. Dame pushed past the few cats that were standing around and stomped over to where Dink and the team were standing.

"What up, my nigga?" Dink said with a smile, holding out his hand to show Dame some love.

"Don't gimme that shit," Dame grumbled, leaving Dink hanging. "That was some bullshit you pulled."

"Fuck is you talking about?" Dink asked, faking confusion.

"Dink, don't play me like that, yo. You know just what the fuck I'm talking about. That muthafucka Titus got hit." Dame paced back and forth a couple of times.

"So? That muthafucka was violating and had to be dealt with. Why you sweatin' it?" Dink asked.

"I don't give a fuck why he died," Dame lied. "I'm tight 'cause he got popped on my block. That shit is wack!"

"First of all, nigga," Dink stepped toward Dame, "watch that bass in ya voice. Second of all, Titus was *your* fucking problem. I shouldn't have had to deal with it."

"Dink, you got no right to get in my business," Dame said. "You know what that makes me look like?"

"Wrong. I got every right when ya business is conflicting with mine. That nigga had to go. End of story." Dink looked away, letting Dame know to drop it.

Dame could feel his rage mounting. He couldn't believe that

Dink was coming at him as if he were a soldier. That didn't sit well with him. In all actuality, he didn't give a shit that Titus was dead. He had planned to kill him soon anyway, but in his own time. Titus was sending quite a bit of money Dame's way with the street tax he was paying.

"Aiight, yo," Dame said, sucking his teeth. "You got that, Dink. You got that." Dame walked away with his hands in his pockets. Part of him wanted to spin around and unload the glock he was carrying, but he knew not to overplay his stroke. Dink would answer for his smart-ass mouth and cocky-ass attitude soon enough. Dame was content to bide his time.

"You better start watching these niggas, Dink," Marco said.

"You ain't lying," Smurf whispered under his breath as they each watched Dame pull off.

AFTER THE DRAMA with Dame earlier, Dink treated Smurf to a lobster dinner in City Island to celebrate yet another successful job. It wasn't often that Dink had the time to cruise the street in his whip and clear his head. He had just dropped Smurf off and was enjoying the late spring night. The wind was still and the stars were trying to shine over the gritty streets. Listening to the smooth grooves of Guy, he spotted her again.

Laci had just come from walking under the railroad trestle. Dink beeped the horn, but she didn't seem to hear it.

"Laci!" he called out, but still she kept walking. Dink checked for oncoming traffic before making a U-turn. He pulled up along-side her and drove slowly, matching her speed. "Laci," he said, wearing a smooth grin. "Where you goin', girl?" She didn't even look in his direction. It was as if she were a zombie. Dink pulled over, got out, and walked up behind her. "Yo, Laci!" He grabbed her arm.

"Get off me!" Snatching her arm from his loose grip, Laci continued her stroll.

"Damn, what's wrong with you, baby?"

She could see that he was going to be persistent; she'd learned her lesson the last time. Trying to get him off her back, she stopped to chat with him for a minute and then be on her way. Dink looked into her eyes and noticed that they were glazed over like two donuts. It was obvious that this was not the same Laci he'd met two weeks ago. Dink's heart pounded in his chest; he knew that all-too-familiar gaze staring back at him. *I know the street ain't got her*, Dink thought to himself.

Laci was in a dreamlike state, looking at him as if she were seeing him for the first time. Finally, she was able to quiet the voices in her head and focus. "Dink?"

"Yeah, it's me, Dink. You aiight? You don't look so good."

Laci gave him a half-ass smile. She wasn't insulted by his comment. She knew she looked like shit. "I'm just trying to get home. My mother is sick," she lied. Dink could see that something wasn't right with Laci. He didn't know her well enough to be able to read her like a book, but he wasn't quite convinced she was telling the truth. Caught up in her physical beauty, his brain and dick wouldn't allow him to analyze her frame of mind.

"Your mother is sick? Then what you doin' around here? Do you know where you at, girl?" Dink said, looking around.

"Yeah, I know," she said, staring down at her shoes. "I just need to get home. I gotta go." She turned around and attempted to walk away, but Dink wasn't going to let her escape without telling him what the real deal was; besides, the longer he looked at her, the more his heart fluttered.

"We've been here before. This time I'm driving you home, no cab, and no trains, just me."

"No... no," she pleaded. "That's okay. You probably have more important things to do." Laci just wanted to be alone with her thoughts and her cravings. Even though she thought Dink was cool, and had saved her life, she didn't feel like being bothered with him at the moment. He was giving her the puppy-dog face. *He is cute,* she thought, *and I know he's feeling me, but I can't. I don't deserve such kindness. He's being nice now, but what about when he finds out I'm a fucking crackhead? I bet he won't be offering me any rides then. Probably won't even look in my direction anymore.*

"You still didn't tell me what you're doing around here." Dink took her by the hand and led her to his car.

"Damn, Dink! I just need to get home," she snapped. "Enough with the interrogation, please."

"Slow down, momma. Ain't nobody trying to get all up in ya shit. I'm just trying to make sure you're good."

"Sorry," she whispered. "I didn't mean to snap. I'm going through something."

"It's cool," he shrugged. "Come on." He opened the car door for her.

"Nah, think I'll take a rain check on this one. Maybe I'll see you later." Laci smiled at Dink and jogged across the street, into the night.

Dink didn't know what put him off more, her nonchalant attitude toward him or the way she left him there speechless. Either way, he was entranced. *I'm gonna make her love me,* he thought.

CHAPTER 14

Growing Pains

MARGARET HAD NOTICED a change in her daughter, and her intuition told her that they needed to have a heart-to-heart. Laci had been keeping late hours and missing school. She refused to go to the doctor or talk with her mother. The first thing Margaret thought of was that Laci might be hiding a pregnancy, although Laci was adamant about not having a boyfriend.

Worry had definitely taken a toll on Laci's mother. She found herself snooping through her daughter's things and even trying to listen in on her phone conversations. It seemed to Margaret that Laci was no longer hanging out with Tonette and her friends. So when Laci came sneaking into the house at three in the morning, Margaret was on the case.

Margaret didn't approach her at first. She wanted to let Laci think she had pulled it off again before she burst her bubble. When she thought Laci had settled in. Margaret went into her bedroom and found her about to change into her pajamas.

"Mom, why are you still up?" Laci said, startled and a little disoriented. Attempting to hide her condition, Laci smoothed her hair and tried to straighten out her clothes. She had been out half the night trying to score a decent blast. Margaret looked Laci up and down and wondered what had happened to her daughter. Laci's hair looked as if she hadn't run a comb through it in days, and her clothes were wrinkled and stained. Considering that Laci didn't even like to wear clothes from last season and would die if her hair was out of place, a red flag went up in Margaret's head.

"Where have you been?" Margaret asked sternly.

"I was out . . . out with a friend."

"Really," Margaret said, with a raised eyebrow. "Which one?"

"Crystal," Laci said, blurting out the first name that came to her mind. "Crystal and I were hanging out in Manhattan."

"That's funny, because Crystal called here for you twice," Margaret said, cleverly playing along with her. "Are you sure it was Crystal you were with?"

"Yeah," Laci continued to lie. "A couple of the other girls were with us, too. Crystal left before the rest of us. She was probably making sure that I got home safely."

Margaret knew her daughter was lying, but she was going to see how far she was willing to go.

"Where did you say you and Quita went again?" Margaret asked.

"I don't remember the name. It was in The Village somewhere."

"I thought you said that you were with Crystal."

"Oh yeah, right," Laci smirked. "I meant to say Crystal. Quita wasn't even there."

"You know, Quita called you too."

"Did she?" Laci said, getting excited. "When? What time? I need to call her back."

Laci headed toward the phone, but her mother stopped her in her tracks, grabbing her by the arm. "Do you know what time it is?" Margaret said, staring at her. "What's wrong with your lips?" Margaret held Laci's face in her hands and observed her.

"Nothing, Ma," Laci said, pulling away.

"Looks like they're scorched . . . like you've been smoking. Are you and your friends smoking?"

"N-o-o-o, Mom!" Laci said, stomping away. "Look, some of the girls smoke, but I don't."

Laci hadn't told the truth since she stepped foot inside the house. In addition to smoking, lying had become a habit she couldn't seem to control. Riding dirty, she excused herself to flush the last flakes of coke she had balled up in her fist. Laci's mother followed her. She stood in the bathroom doorway and saw her struggle to stand upright.

"Laci?" Margaret whispered.

"I'm trying to use the bathroom." Laci went to close the door.

"Talk to me, Laci, please." Margaret placed her hand on the door to stop it from closing. "What's going on, baby? Come on, Laci. You know that you've always been able to talk to me. That will never change."

"Fine, Mom. Cool. We'll talk," Laci said, trying to get rid of her. "Just give me a second to use the bathroom." Margaret removed her hand, allowing Laci to close and lock the door. Laci held her hand over the toilet and hesitated. There were only a few flakes left, but it was enough to numb her pain. Laci ran her index finger through it, then rubbed the coke across her gums.

"Laci, are you okay in there?" Margaret asked through the closed door.

Laci closed her eyes in shame. No way could she could poison herself while her mother stood on the other side of the door. She took the little bit of coke that was left, poured it in the toilet, and flushed it. It hurt like hell to watch her get-high disappear, but this was just the beginning of the heavy price she'd have to pay for living a double life.

"I'm okay, Mom," Laci called back. "I'll be out in a second."

Laci washed her face, splashed water on her messy hair, and slicked it down with her hands. She wanted to give the appearance that she had it together, but the mirror didn't lie. Laci opened the bathroom door and found that her mother hadn't budged.

"Laci, I'm so worried about you." Margaret followed her to her room. "What's going on? You missed the last three weeks of school. Graduation is next week and you haven't even begun to prepare for your trip to Puerto Rico, or college for that matter."

"Mom, I'm just tired," Laci said, rubbing her forehead. "You know, ever since I caught the flu I haven't been myself. As far as school goes, you know the worst grade I've ever gotten since kindergarten was an A-minus. I'm graduating. Don't worry about it. Everything is fine."

Margaret wasn't naïve; she knew there was something more to Laci's story than what she was saying. "Are you cold?" she asked, touching the goose bumps on her arm. "You're shivering."

"No, I'm fine," Laci said, examining her arms. "I don't know why I'm trembling like this. Maybe I'm cold. I don't know, Mommy." Laci began to laugh, even though things were far from funny right now.

"All right, Laci," her mother said, sounding as though she

was about to throw in the towel. "Like I said, I worry about you. You've been hanging out a lot and I can tell that you haven't been eating much. You have to start eating square meals. You don't want to fall dead out there, do you?"

"Don't you think that's a little extreme, Mom?" Laci said. "I'm not gonna die just because I'm not stuffing my face every five minutes. Besides, I do eat."

"We need to start taking better care of you. I want you in tip-top shape for your graduation. Your father would be so proud of you. I know he already is." Margaret hid her sadness with a smile. She paused. It was time to get to the point. "Laci, are you taking any drugs?" She couldn't find an easier way to ask this difficult question.

"Why would you ask me that?" Laci asked defensively. "Do I look like I'm taking anything?"

Margaret dropped her head and sighed. "Answer my question, Laci."

"Mom, I can't believe you," Laci said, flipping the script. "You know how important fitting in with my friends is to me. Is it because I've been hanging out a little more than usual? That doesn't mean I'm doing drugs."

"This just doesn't sound like you, Laci."

"Well, it *is* me, Mom. People change."

"I'm so disappointed in you right now." Laci's mother's words were filled with emotion.

"Mom, I swear to you," Laci said, walking over to her mother and gently placing her hands on her shoulders. "You have to believe me."

"Okay," Margaret said with a sigh, giving in, but still not feeling totally at ease about the situation. "If you say so, then I have to believe you. Here, let me help you into bed."

"Mom, I'm almost eighteen," Laci said, throwing her a friendly look. "I can put my own self to bed. I'm not a baby."

Margaret quickly pulled Laci to her bosom and hugged her. "You will always be my baby. Sleep well, Laci. I'll make you a big breakfast in the morning. I want you to stay home and rest up this weekend. No excuses. And you're going to school on Monday?"

"I don't know, Mom . . . I'll try," Laci said.

"No, Laci. You *are* going to school. If you aren't able to go to school, then you sure in hell shouldn't be able to run the streets. Maybe I should call Dr. Stevens and tell him to make a house call, since you're so sick."

"Fine, Mom, I'll go to school on Monday."

"That's what I thought. Good night, baby." Margaret smiled.

"Good night," Laci said as she watched her mother head toward the door.

Laci watched her mother leave her room and closed the door behind her. It eased her mind to know that she had gotten her mother off her tail. Waiting until she swore she heard her mother's head touch her pillow, she picked up the phone and quickly began to dial.

"Hello, Quita," Laci whispered into the receiver after Quita had answered the phone half-asleep. "It's me, Laci. How much money do I need?"

CHAPTER 15

Family Ties

FRANTIC, LACI SEARCHED for a place to light up after exiting the nearly empty subway station. She couldn't wait to smoke the rest of Dame's work, but she wouldn't dare do it on the streets. If the police rolled on her, they might take her drugs. She had one other option, but she didn't like it. Not long ago, a friend of a new smoke buddy hipped her to a spot where she could get her mind right if she was ever in the area. Laci couldn't remember the building number, but she'd know it if she saw it.

After crossing her way through Harlem, Laci found the building she was looking for. It was right off of 137th Street and Seventh Avenue. She hiked up the stairs of the front stoop and headed for the door. Finally, Laci had somewhere to smoke in peace. But just when she thought she was home free, she ran into her uncle. *Where in the fuck did he come from?* she wondered. *I haven't seen him in forever and a day.* The only reason she even recognized him was because he was the spitting image of her own father.

"Laci?" he asked in shock.

"Uncle Sonny?" Laci replied.

"What the hell you doin' around here, baby?" his eyes begged to know. "Yo' momma know you hanging on a dope block?"

Laci smiled innocently. "Hey, Uncle Sonny. I was just coming from a friend's house. She lives in this building."

Sonny looked at Laci as if she were crazy. She was standing in front of a dope spot trying to match wits with a professional liar. Sonny had been a junkie for more years than she had been alive. He could tell by the way she was fidgeting that something was wrong. He looked into his niece's eyes and saw her monkey.

"What's the real deal?" he asked. "I've been around for a long time. You think I don't know one of my own?"

"Uncle Sonny," she began. Laci thought for a few seconds. "Why would you think that? Do I look like a drug addict? I'm just tired. It's late. And, what are *you* doing here?"

Sonny stared at his niece, trying to get a line on her. Truth was he had been a dope addict since 1965. It cost him everything, most importantly his relationship with his mother and his brother, Jay. When confronted by his family, Sonny left and never came back. He wasn't there for his mother's funeral, or for his brother's college graduation, marriage, or death. Margaret was big on family and for years snuck behind her husband's back, sending Sonny money and keeping tabs on him. It was she who paid for his rehab and set him up with a boarding house. Clean for a year, Sonny had woke up that morning with a jones he couldn't shake. After a day of work at the supermarket, he traveled to his old hangout to see his old friends, but mostly to score his first hit in a while. Seeing Laci squashed all that.

"What's your friend's apartment number?" he asked intuitively.

"Uncle Sonny," she said, sucking her teeth, "I'm not going to tell you that so you can go bothering her, trying to check up on me. It's late and people need their sleep. Speaking of which, I better get going myself."

"C'mon," he said, putting his arm around her. "I can't let you go off by yourself. I'll go with you."

"No, Uncle Sonny," she protested. "I'm okay. I'm good. No need for you to do that. You just go on."

"Why you gettin' all excited?" Sonny asked suspiciously.

"Like I said, I'm just tired. Can't wait to go home and get me some sleep." Laci let out a fake yawn and stretched.

Sonny knew damn well that Laci wasn't telling the truth and that she didn't have any friends in this area. He was looking around to see if there was anything that would give him an idea of what she was really doing there when a known, local crackhead walked by and greeted her by name.

"Hey, Laci," the crackhead said.

"Hey, Angel," Laci replied as Angel strutted away, switching her ass like she was the baddest bitch on the block and always would be. Laci had heard that back in the day she was the finest girl around the way. But now she was a strawberry . . . a bum.

"I gotta go," Laci said. She lowered her head and walked off. Sonny called behind her, but Laci kept going.

"Hold up," Sonny said, catching up with Laci and grabbing her by the hand. He looked down, closed his eyes, and took a deep breath. He didn't want to look in his niece's eyes again. He didn't want to see that look, but he had to.

"What is it, Uncle Sonny? I gotta get home."

Sonny lifted his head and looked into Laci's eyes. "Looking into your eyes is like looking in a mirror, girl. I had that same look, too, back in the 'sixties when I started using," Sonny said in a deep, sincere tone. Laci moved her lips in an attempt to respond, but Sonny raised his free hand to keep her from speaking. "Don't talk. Just listen. I know what these streets can do to a girl like you, Laci. I've seen it. Hell, I'm a grown man, and I know what these streets have done to me. Some things I'm too ashamed to even admit . . . can't even face myself sometimes. And I don't blame your daddy for havin' nothin' to do with me."

"Uncle Sonny—"

"No, no, girl. Let me talk." Sonny paused for a moment. "I know I ain't been in your life enough to be telling you a damn thang. But I'm gonna tell you anyway." Sonny shook his head and tightened his lips to control his emotions. "Don't do it, Laci," he said, moving his hand up and down with each syllable while Laci's was still cupped inside it. "Don't become like your Uncle Sonny here. You'll have nothing. You'll *be* nothing. You're far too pretty and smart. I know my brother ain't raised no fool. He was a strong man, and proud. That's how I know you're strong, too, Laci. You're strong enough to get out now."

"But, Uncle Sonny, I don't know what you're talking a—"

"Look at me, Laci. I'm an old man. You think you can outslick a slicker? Battin' them pretty little eyes might work on ya mama, but not on me. I know these streets, and the streets don't lie."

Laci put her head down and pulled her hand away from Sonny's.

"Unh-uh," he said, lifting Laci's head by her chin. "Don't go puttin' your head down now. It ain't too late to beat this thing. Go to your momma. She loves you, Laci." Sonny paused. "Your daddy loved you too; you were his heart. Ain't no man gon' love you like yo' daddy. And see, when a man loves you, he's got to appreciate you at your worst in order to appreciate you at your best. Remember that with any man, Laci. But you also need to remember who don't love you, and that's the streets. They mean. And so are those who belong to the streets."

Laci had heard enough. She knew her uncle meant well, but getting high meant better. "I hear you, Uncle Sonny, but it ain't even like that with me. Look, I gotta get going." Laci gave her uncle a quick peck on the cheek and ran off.

"Laci!" he shouted. "Laci!" Laci disappeared into the darkness.

Being an addict himself, Sonny knew all of the early signs of addiction. And he didn't like what he was seeing right now. It was bad enough that he had fucked his life up with drugs, but he couldn't bear to watch his niece go through the same thing. He had failed his mother and his brother, but the least he could do was save Laci.

"HELLO," MARGARET ANSWERED.

"Hi, it's me, Sonny."

"Hey now." Margaret sounded chipper, but Sonny knew that was a front.

"Well, I got to get back to work soon. I'm on a break, but I need to talk to you about—"

"Laci?" Margaret said, her voice trembling.

"I don't want to jump to any conclusions, but something's not right. I ran into her the other night in Harlem." Sonny took the phone from his ear and put it on his chest. Nothing sounded worse to his ears than a mother's cry. This was the cry he had constantly tried to avoid hearing many years earlier, and now here it was again.

"Sonny, you still there?" Margaret asked after he hadn't responded for a few moments. Sonny put the phone back to his ear. "Sonny?" Margaret repeated.

"Yeah, sis. I'm here," he said, sniffling. "She didn't look right. I mean, she still looked like my beautiful niece, but there was something in her eyes, Margaret. It was a look I've seen before."

"Where?" Margaret feared the answer.

Sonny sighed. "She was in a place she didn't need to be."

"No, I mean where had you seen the look before?"

Sonny paused. It killed him to say the words that were about to roll off his tongue, but he knew he had to. "In the mirror."

Margaret began to whimper even harder. Her cries cut like a knife. They were digging old wounds in Sonny—very deep wounds. It seemed as if they were bleeding and would never stop. Sonny felt as though he were hemorrhaging.

"Oh, my God, Sonny," Margaret cried. "Oh, my God."

"Hey, hey," Sonny said, trying to soothe her. "C'mon now, sis. I'll take care of it. In fact, I'm already on it."

"Thank you, Sonny," Margaret said, regaining her composure. "But in your condition, I don't want you in the streets either. Leave this to me."

"No problem. She's my family, too. You and Laci are all I have left. If I hear anything I'll let you know."

"I appreciate it. You know she's supposed to go away to school this fall. I'm just so afraid that she's going to mess everything up for herself."

"Don't worry, Margaret," Sonny assured her. "We won't let her end up like me."

"I'd die before I let that happen."

CHAPTER 16

That's What Friends Are For

QUITA WAS HARDLY surprised the first time Laci called her. Word was getting around about the new fine-ass crackhead hitting the block. Quita knew only one person who fit the description. After Quita and Tonette went to blows, she had lain low for a while putting in work for Dame.

Laci didn't really know Quita that well. She'd met her a couple of times when she first started hanging out with the S.B.B. and remembered that Quita was always smiling and nice to her. Not fully a part of the crew, Laci never really found out the truth about Quita and why she'd left, but whenever she saw her around she made sure to say hello.

Laci made small talk, but Quita knew there was more to her call. Tired of going back and forth, Laci finally asked Quita if she wanted to hang out. She was all too pleased when Quita accepted. She told herself that she just needed someone to talk to and nothing more.

Quita gave Laci a sisterly hug when she arrived at her house. Laci had never gotten a hug from any one of her so-called homegirls. She thought that she might have finally found a friend.

"Girl, I was so surprised when you called me," Quita lied. "It's been ages."

Laci smiled. "I know. I figured I'd see what you were up to. I felt like a change of pace."

"I know that's right," Quita said, pulling out a bag of weed. "You know I ain't the judgmental type, but I don't know what you see in them low-life bitches you run with. Why you think I left?"

"They're all right," Laci said with a shrug.

"Bullshit. Them some jealous hoes and you know it. Come on, now, Laci. Look at how them bitches treat you. They act all funny 'cause they're jealous. Tell me I'm wrong," Quita said, waiting on a response that she never got.

Laci knew that Quita was right and that everything all boiled down to jealousy. Why else would they always try to tear her down? She had always shown them so much love and they tried to flip the script on her at every turn. Quita was right. Fuck them bitches.

Quita continued to roll the blunt while Laci silently listened to her bash Tonette and the rest of the crew. Seeing the weed increased Laci's urge to get high, but she was able to maintain her cool. It was when Quita pulled out the cocaine that almost made her lose it. Being the virgin she was, she would have hated for her first orgasm ever to be right there on Quita's couch, but the sight of the cocaine made her want to nut all over herself.

Quita opened the tinfoil and began to slowly sprinkle the powder over the weed. Laci's mouth literally started to water. Quita finished rolling the joint and lit it. The smell wasn't quite the same as Laci remembered it, but still very similar. Quita saw the weakness in Laci's eyes and decided to play on it.

"I would offer," Quita said, slowly blowing out the smoke, "but I know you don't get down."

"I'll hit it," Laci blurted out.

"What?" Quita said, pulling her head back to get a good look at Laci.

"I've tried some weed once or twice," Laci said.

"Sister girl, this ain't just weed. This is a woo. I don't know if you're ready to get this high."

"I'll try it, just this once," Laci said with greed in her eyes.

"Okay," Quita said, passing the blunt. She made it a point to hold it just out of Laci's reach so that she'd have to stretch to get it.

Laci could already taste it. Her hands were shaking as she brought it to her mouth and inhaled deeply. Her hands stopped shaking when the smoke entered her system. She didn't hear "Cloud Nine" this time, but she felt normal again.

Quita sat across from Laci, who was now enjoying her high with her eyes closed. She could tell when she first saw Laci that she needed a fix; whether she knew it or not, she had gone past the point of chipping and was developing a full-blown habit.

Quickly, Quita turned Laci on to the fast track. She taught her that a crack high was cheap, but a coke high was better. Laci alternated whenever the mood struck her.

She and Quita continued to get higher than high for a whole week straight (even on the day of her high school graduation)—

snorting and smoking up anything they could get their hands on. It was to the point where Laci wasn't even mixing the shit anymore. She was straight-up basing.

TONETTE AND HER crew were inside Crown Fried Chicken, watching the day go by. Shaunna was sitting on a milk crate complaining about stomach cramps, Crystal was on a pay phone arguing with Dink, and Monique stared out the window. She had been unusually quiet the entire day. Tonette peeped it and wondered what the hell was going on.

"Anybody seen Laci lately?" Tonette asked, pouring hot sauce on her chicken wings and french fries.

Crystal, who had just hung up the phone on Dink, replied, "I ain't seen her since the other day. I was shopping on 145th and I saw her walk past the window. Bitch is probably somewhere getting high," she said, laughing.

"You need to quit," Tonette told her.

"Stop acting like you wasn't wit' it, bitch," Shaunna said, rolling her eyes at Tonette. "You were the one who set off the whole shit."

"Yeah, well, we was all wit' it the first time," Tonette said.

"But you kept the shit up," Crystal added. "That girl could be really twisted behind that."

"Fuck that bitch," Monique cut in, angry at the whole world right now. "Serves her right for wanting to be so down."

"I still don't think it was cool," Shaunna said.

Crystal sighed, taking in Shaunna's words. "I don't know. Maybe you're right."

"But you didn't seem to feel like that when she was all up in Dink's face," Tonette reminded Crystal.

"That called for an ass-whipping, not a fucking addiction," Crystal snapped.

"Whatever," Tonette replied. "What we doin' tonight?"

"Shit, this lil' muthafucka is kicking my ass," Shaunna said, rubbing her stomach.

"Ain't nobody include yo' ass in the equation," Tonette teased her.

"Fuck you," Shaunna shot back. "When I drop my load, it's on again."

Their exchange was interrupted when Dink and Marco entered the chicken joint. Dink was his usual dapper self, wearing a pair of black Guess jeans and some white and green Fila sneakers. He spotted the girls, walked over, and kissed Crystal on the cheek.

"What up, ma?" he said with a smile, as if they hadn't just finished arguing on the phone.

"Don't try to be sweet now," she snapped. "You wasn't sweet a minute ago on the phone." Crystal had hung up on Dink because of his stink attitude. He acted as if he had better things to do than to talk to her.

"Stop acting like that," Dink said, hugging her. "You know how you like to call when I'm handling business."

"Well, since you're handling business, can I get some money?" Crystal stuck out her hand.

He sucked his teeth. "Damn." Dink wasn't used to Crystal just coming straight out like that and asking for ends. "I ain't even been in this muthafucka for two minutes and you're begging."

"Don't try to play me, Dink," she barked. "I hardly see you anymore, and when I do, you're distracted."

"Look, I ain't got time for this shit, Crystal. Take this," he huffed, handing her a fifty. "Holla at me later." Dink walked away and joined Marco at the counter to place his order.

"What the fuck I'ma do with this?" she asked loudly enough for Dink to hear her, but he didn't even bother to turn around. "That's aiight," she mumbled. "You ain't the only nigga handling business."

CHAPTER 17

It Takes Two

DINK HAD BEEN lenient in how he allowed Dame to run his business. He let him operate independently and wasn't constantly looking over his shoulder. He trusted Dame with a lot, and he wasn't handling his shit. It was high time that he put his affairs in order.

Driving around the turf for hours looking for his soldier turned out to be a bust, but it did produce Laci, and Dink wasn't mad at that at all. He ran into her in almost the exact same place as before, but this time it was clear to him why she was in the area.

Dink pulled up beside her, and this time she acknowledged him immediately.

"What's the deal, baby? You following me?" Laci asked with a beautiful smile.

"Maybe," he said in a flirtatious tone. "Would it be a problem if I was?"

"Depends on what you're following me for," she replied with a wink.

"I'll make a note of that, ma. Say, how come I don't see you over at the house anymore? Fuck you been up to?"

Laci opened Dink's car door. She hopped in, wearing a big smile, and said, "Aren't you the inquisitive one?" Dink would sit there counting her teeth all day if he could. Her smile was just magnetizing. But aside from the smile, Laci was starting to let herself go. The beautiful curly locks that he remembered were no more. She pretty much repped the lazy-do—a pulled-back ponytail that hadn't even been taken out to be redone in a minute. It was obvious that it had gotten the slick-down hand job by the pieces that were out of place. Laci still wore the classy little name-brand hook-ups, but it looked like she had been to a dozen sleepovers in them.

Dink scanned Laci, and his face clearly showed his uneasiness with her condition.

For the most part, she was still cute. Shit, she looked better than most females in the hood did on their best day. But seeing her again only confirmed the rumors. However, that spark he felt the day he met her at Crystal's house was still there.

"So, seriously, Laci," Dink said with sincerity, "what have you really been up to?"

"Do I look like a book to you?" Laci asked calmly.

"Huh?" Dink asked, obviously confused.

"Do I look like a book to you?" Laci changed her profile a couple of times for him to examine.

"No," he snickered.

Laci became serious. "Then stop trying to read me, baby. I'm good."

Dink just smiled.

There was so much Dink wanted to say, but he couldn't seem to focus. He had so much on his plate that his feelings for Laci seemed secondary. He started to put it off for another time, but if he didn't say what he wanted to, he might never do it.

"Laci," he said looking into her eyes, "I hope I don't make a fool of myself by saying this, but fuck it."

"What? Just say it."

"Ever since the time when I saw you at Crystal's house, I wondered what it would be like to have . . ." Dink started laughing. "Oh, this is some crazy shit. What the fuck am I doing, yo?"

Dink paused and melted when Laci smiled. Then he manned up. "I'm feeling you, girl, and I can't help but wonder what it would be like to have you as my own."

"Your own what?" Laci asked, dumbfounded.

Dink jerked his head back and gave her a puzzled look.

"I'm just kidding," Laci said, smiling again. "I know what you mean." Laci hadn't smiled so much since she could remember. No one had ever made her smile like that before. But she'd snuck in that little joke because she really didn't know how to respond to Dink. His statement had thrown her off. She knew Dink looked at her in a more-than-friendly way, but she thought it was just a physical attraction. She could have easily gotten into him if he hadn't been Crystal's man. She wanted to tell him that, but she played it cool. She, too, had so much going on in her life.

"You probably say that to all the girls, Dink," she said, continuing to play around. "By the way, how's ya girl?"

"I haven't really been seeing a whole lot of Crystal," Dink said, hating that Laci spoiled the moment by mentioning her name. "She's probably got her hands full anyway."

"Yeah, well, I don't see too much of her either. I just haven't been in the mood to hang out with the girls these days. What's your excuse?"

"I'm not in the mood for her either." Dink took a deep breath and stretched. "I'm thinking about moving on."

"Is that right?"

"Yeah. People grow apart, ya know?" Dink paused for a second. "Listen, I know that you and Crystal are friends or whatever, but I don't believe in wasted opportunities, so enough of talking about her. I'm trying to see about *you*, ma."

"So what they say about you is right, huh?" Laci said in somewhat of a sensual tone. "You do run a good game." Laci looked down and started picking at her fingernails. "All guys like you do is scam on women. I know your kind," she said, sucking her teeth.

Dink was fully animated as he explained himself. "Look at me," he said lifting Laci's face by the chin and turning it toward him so that they were eye to eye. "I put this on everything. You're like this perfect chick out of a movie or some shit. And I'm..." Dink searched for the right words. "I'm a hustler, baby. I ain't go to college or nothin' like that, and unlike yourself, I don't plan on going. I know you come from money, went to private schools and all that. I can't compete with that. But as far as the money part, I'm good. We wouldn't have to worry about finances."

"All of your money is dirty, Dink," Laci said in a serious tone, still looking him in the eye. "And you and I both know what happens to dirty money." Laci paused to let him think on it. "It gets washed away. I mean, for real though. You can't buy a house with it. You can't even walk into a bank and get an account, so you can't even save it. Hell, you can't do shit with your kind of money but burn it on the streets."

"That's where you're wrong," Dink said.

"How so?"

Dink licked his lips and leaned in close to Laci. "Don't you worry your pretty head about that. I got that all figured out," he said before sitting back in position. "We won't even have to worry about that."

"What's this *we* stuff?" Laci asked.

"Because ain't no 'I' in team, Laci. You and me—us. We could be a team."

Laci looked at Dink sideways, shook her head, then looked out the window. "Ain't no *I* in team, huh?"

"That's what I said."

Laci turned back to Dink. "Ain't no *we* either." She let out a chuckle.

"You keep playing all you want, girl, but I'm for real."

"Dink, you have a girlfriend, so the fact that you are sitting here saying all of this, with me knowing you have a girlfriend, lets me know what type of man you really are. No offense, but if you're doing this type of stuff to Crystal, why should I believe that you ain't gonna do it to me?"

"Because I'm being real with you from the jump," Dink said.

"But I'm not the one you need to be real with right now—Crystal is," Laci said. "If you kept shit so real, then she would know how you supposedly feel about me."

Dink sighed. "It ain't no *supposed* feeling. I'm putting my shit on the line telling you this. And you know it must be real, considering—" Dink caught himself. He almost slipped up and said something that might have hurt Laci's feelings. He truly didn't want to take it there. Besides, he wasn't one to go on rumor alone. He hadn't heard the shit from Laci, so a part of him still wanted to believe in something other than the obvious. Dink understood that people sometimes went through rough times, and this could be one of those times for Laci. He would love to be there for her, to see her through—if she'd let him.

"Fuck it. I see I'm wasting my breath and have probably just made a complete fool out of myself," he said.

"Then that's a good thing," Laci replied softly. "Means you got love in your heart."

"What?" Dink said.

"They say a person only makes a fool out of themselves for love," Laci said.

"Or for money," Dink said, looking deeply into her eyes.

Laci turned away and stared out of the window. She felt as though Dink had her numbers and was just waiting for her to yell Bingo!

"I really dig the way you came at me and all, Dink. But the you and me, and the 'we' thing . . . it ain't a reality. I could never be with you, Dink."

"Why? Why not, Laci?"

Laci fought back tears. "Isn't it obvious, Dink? You deal drugs and I . . ." she paused. "I'm friends with your girlfriend." Laci's thoughts began to race. She wanted so badly to spill the beans to Dink. She needed help, but she bitched up. She just couldn't.

"Laci, first of all, I told you that I'm cutting Crystal off. She's not what I'm looking for and if I'm going to have a woman in my life, it's gonna be the one I really want. And as far as the drug shit goes, I think I already know what time it is with you, Laci."

Laci looked at Dink in shock. She turned away in humiliation as tears flowed down her cheeks. "Guess I do look like a book after all," Laci sobbed.

Dink put his hand on her shoulder. He felt so sick inside that she was confirming that shit—just absolutely sick. He gritted his teeth hard to maintain his emotions. He wasn't tripping over Laci, but he had seen the best of them go down and he refused to watch the same thing happen to her.

"Did you think I wouldn't find out, Laci, doing what I do?" Dink said. "I just can't figure out why and how you got into this."

Laci bowed her head in shame. In all her running and having fun, she'd never even considered how many people would find out, simply from word on the street. Dink was one of the biggest narcotics distributors in the Bronx. Laci tried to do her thing outside of her borough, but news always traveled from hood to hood.

Laci could feel Dink's eyes burning a hole through her as he waited on a response.

"Dink, don't look at me, please," Laci cried.

"It's cool, ma," Dink said, running his hand over her hair.

"No, don't touch me." Laci jerked away. "You don't wanna touch me, trust me," she said, starting to feel sorry for herself. "It's not my fault," she sobbed.

Dink bit down on his lip and tried to maintain his composure, but what he really wanted to do was take her in his arms and hold her. He never wanted to let her go. He wanted to keep her from slipping even deeper. "What do you mean it's not your fault, Laci? You gotta step up to bat before you can even think about changing the situation."

"No, you don't understand. It's really not my fault," Laci said emotionally.

"Somebody forced it on you or something? Talk to me," Dink insisted.

Laci scratched at her ponytail. "Not exactly," she sighed. "You just don't understand. I don't want to smoke, but shit just got so crazy. I tried to back away from it, but the shit just kept calling me back. I don't know what to do," Laci cried. "I don't know what to do, Dink. Oh, my God."

Laci felt as though a weight had been lifted from her shoulders. She had finally been able to just sit down and tell somebody. There was so much more she wanted to tell Dink, though, like how the mere thought of getting high made her squirm. She thought about the rocks she had on her at that very moment and how much better she would feel if she smoked them. Talking to Dink had made her forget about them at first, but that was only short-term. The stones were now humming in a low tone, but they would soon be singing soprano.

Dink took Laci's hand into his. Even after hearing it from the horse's mouth, that Laci Johnson was a crack addict, he still couldn't resist her. He simply saw her as a diamond in the rough. She just needed someone to shine her up a little bit. Dink had been in the game long enough to understand the addiction to crack. But with crack being a mental drug, each person had his or her own catalyst for getting hooked. He needed to understand Laci's before he could help her. He needed to know the driving force behind it. He'd heard the saying about not being able to turn a ho into a housewife. But here it was, 1989, and no one had yet come to any conclusions about crackheads.

Dink exhaled. "Tell me all about your addiction, Laci. What made you want to use crack for the very first time?"

Laci was compelled to shed all of her bad skin in front of Dink. She began to air all her dirty laundry with little hesitation. Laci recounted all of the summer's events for Dink. She told him about the laced weed and a host of other shit he wasn't aware of. On one hand, he felt like crying with her. But on the other hand, he felt like killing everyone involved.

"Sons of bitches!" Dink roared as he beat down on his dashboard. "I could kill them dead, all of 'em."

"I've felt like that, too," Laci said, not realizing that she had lifted her hand to run her fingers through his hair. "All I can do is pray that God takes care of them for what they did. That's all you can do, too." Laci forced herself to smile.

Dink looked at her closely, and now he could see the hurt behind the smile. Now she wasn't fooling anybody.

He closed his eyes for a moment as Laci continued stroking his hair. Then he opened his eyes and held her head in his hands before placing it on his shoulder. She felt so much better talking to someone. She'd just never thought in a million years that it would be Dink, especially the way she had played him off the last time he tried to look out for her. He had every right to condemn her and push her away, but he had been very understanding.

Laci and Dink exchanged long glances. He took his fingers and wiped her tears away. He then kissed her softly on the lips and brushed her hair with his hand.

In a short time, Laci and Dink connected like they had never done with any other person in their lives. In just a matter of a few hours, they really did become a team.

LACI HELD ONTO Dink, it seemed, for dear life. She basked in the attention he gave her, and her body language revealed that all of her defenses were down. She wanted more, but she reluctantly showed restraint for the moment.

"I feel so much better," Laci said to Dink as she straightened out her clothes. "You're the first person I've been able to talk to about this. I used to talk to my mom about everything. She was like my best friend—pillow fights and all. But this . . . this would have killed her."

Dink nodded in agreement.

"Seems like now you know a lot about me, but I know nothing about you," Laci said. "Tell me about your family."

Dink became tense. "I don't have no family."

"Really? No mother? No father?"

"Nah. From what I was told when I was little, my mother was an addict and gave me to a pimp named Bruce Ward in exchange for drugs. I grew up crazy, and the only saving grace I had, even though it was short-lived, was my cousin, Fred. Fred was Bruce's bottom bitch's son, and we instantly formed a bond like brothers. But he was an insecure dude, and deep down he hated me."

"Why did he hate you?"

"I don't even know, man," Dink said, shaking his head. "I guess he had a lot of reasons for hating me."

"That's sad, Dink. How did you deal with it?"

Dink smiled confidently. "By becoming somebody. No matter what, I wouldn't be broken. No matter what anybody did, they couldn't make me fall."

"You're a strong man. I guess that's why I feel so safe with you."

"You should," he said as he kissed her forehead. "I'd never let anything happen to you."

"You mean it?" she asked.

"Of course. I'm gonna look out for you if you let me."

"I'll think about it," she teased. Laci suddenly paused and stared into Dink's eyes. For the first time she noticed how pretty they were. Her laughter faded as she melted in them.

"What's wrong?" he asked.

"Your eyes," she said, mesmerized. "You have very beautiful eyes." Laci gently touched the side of his face and ran her fingers across his eyelids, placing a soft kiss on each of them.

Dink slowly opened his eyes and looked at Laci. "Is it just me, girl, or does it seem like we've known each other forever?"

"It's not just you," Laci said in a heavy whisper, trying to control her lustful breathing. "I feel it too, baby."

"Girl, you playin' with fire," Dink said.

"I can stand the pain of a burn," Laci assured him. "I've endured worse."

"I'm for real, Laci. This is not a game."

"So am I."

"So what are we gon' do, ma?"

"I don't know, Dink," Laci said, settling back over on the passenger side. "There's still Crystal to deal with."

"That's a done deal. But you know, if we gonna get down, your lifestyle has got to change."

Laci looked at Dink as if he was the pot calling the kettle black. "And *your* lifestyle, Dink?"

"Tell me what you need from me, ma, and it's done."

Laci sighed and tried to find the right words. "If I asked you to stop hustling, Dink—"

"I see where you're going with this," he said, cutting her off.

"I got a habit, you know," Laci continued. "I already admitted that to you. And how am I gonna roll with you if you're supplying? That's like letting a drunk be a bartender, a fat person owning a bakery."

Dink laughed. "Girl, you crazy." He paused to look at Laci and saw that she was dead serious. "Look. I'll tell you what. We'll work on bettering both our lifestyles together. Deal?"

Laci didn't know how much of what Dink was saying was real and just how much of it was bullshit. But she did know that she liked what she was hearing. "You got a deal," she said.

"Let's make it official," Dink said, holding out his hand.

Laci looked at him as if she didn't know what he was talking about. The more she thought about it, parting with her rock didn't seem like much of an option. She wasn't ready—not yet. Her insecurity showed when she looked into his eyes—those eyes that revealed so much. They told her that it was okay to be weak, for he would be her strength. They told her that it was okay to crave, for he would be her fix. His eyes told her that it was okay to believe in him, and maybe someday to even love him.

Dink shook his hand as if to ask Laci if she was going to leave him hanging.

Laci stared at Dink's hand for a few more seconds before pulling out her ziplock baggie. She stared at the contents. She and her little torturers had been through quite a bit, but the road would have to end somewhere. Laci placed the bag of rocks in Dink's hand.

He looked at Laci with hope in his eyes. Then he looked around, opened the car door, emptied the rocks onto the ground, and stomped every last one to nothingness.

Tears welled up in Laci's eyes, but she knew it was for the better. Kicking her addiction was going to be a bitch, but she wouldn't have to do it alone.

Dink caught the tears that fell from her eyes with his fingertips. He hugged her tightly. It was the first time Laci had hugged a man since her father died. For the first time since his death, she felt safe.

CHAPTER 18

She's Gotta Have It

"YEAH," DAME SAID, answering the phone just like any hustler would. It didn't matter if you called him at four in the morning or four at night, he'd be up hustling.

"Hey, it's your girl, Quita," Quita said, sitting back blowing smoke. "It's taken some doing, but I finally got the bitch exactly where we want her."

LACI'S EYES DARTED about, scanning apartment buildings, parked cars, and people who knew she was out of her element. She knew where she was, but she kept asking herself what the fuck she was doing there. She wanted to turn around and leave, but the promise of the get-high was too tempting.

"Does Dame live over here, Quita?" Laci nervously scratched her neck.

Quita snatched Laci by her wrist as if she were being a disobedient child. "Just follow me and stop asking so many fuckin' questions. Stop being paranoid and come the fuck on. My man ain't gon' wait all day."

"He's just going to give me some, right?" Laci questioned. "I mean, I don't have any money right now, but I'm good for it."

Quita didn't say a word. Her expression and tight grip on Laci's arm said it all. She knew that bringing Laci around would cause all of the men on the street to inquire and hold them up, so she made a conscious effort to avoid them. There was no need to fully expose Laci to this world—at least not yet. For now it was better that she remained nothing more than a rumor. And Quita had already violated one of her man's cardinal rules. Being late would double her punishment, and Dame was hard on his bitches. As the two approached the building's back entrance, Quita gave specific instructions.

"Listen, don't act stupid while you up here, Laci. I'm doin' you a favor. Do exactly what he say and we won't have no problems. Everything will go smooth."

"Okay," Laci said. "I trust you, Quita. You're not like the other girls. I know you're not going to let anything happen to me, right?"

"Nah, you my girl. I got your back."

They were lucky to catch a ride on the rickety elevator, being that it was more of a young person's sex and weed hangout than a means to transport passengers from floor to floor. Waiting to reach the fifth floor, Quita leaned against the back of the elevator. She focused on how beautiful Laci was—her hair, skin, frame, and facial features—even in her present condition.

By the time the ding for the fifth floor sounded, disgust was visible in Quita's dark brown pupils. She unbuttoned Laci's jacket. "Leave this shit open. He need to see." Laci became nervous, and she began rambling senseless things while continually straightening her already tucked-in shirt. If not before, Quita knew that the expected hit now had her completely bananas.

"What the hell are you talkin' about, Laci?" Quita said as the elevator stopped. "Don't you fall apart on me. We here now, so get your shit together. You ready?"

"Huh?" Laci replied, dazed.

"Huh, hell! I asked you, are you ready?"

Laci's eyes were empty and she stood like a zombie while Quita tried to shake enough life into her to get her to walk out of the elevator before the door closed.

Laci snapped out of her stupor and shoved Quita off of her with attitude. "Stop shaking me, damn it! I hear you."

"Bitch," Quita said, putting her fingers in Laci's face. She thought about beating Laci's ass for biting the hand that fed her. But now wasn't the time. "G-i-r-r-r-l, you don't know. Just bring your ass."

Quita led Laci to a rusty blue door, knocked on it, and waited. Laci's constant pacing made her remember how bad she wanted to get high before she paced herself and became a heavyweight. In Laci's case, Dame had been rationing out the powder to Quita until she was able to turn Laci out completely.

After what seemed like forever, Dame answered the door. He wore a black bathrobe and was sipping a Guinness. He looked at Laci and made a funny face. He'd never personally met her, but he would have known who she was had he passed her on the street based on all the talk.

"Who the fuck is this?" Dame asked as if he didn't already know.

"This is the girl I was telling you about," Quita said, walking into the apartment and pulling Laci behind her. "This is Laci."

"What up, girl?" Dame said, licking his lips.

"Hi," Laci said shyly. She began feeling a little guilty about being around Quita and Dame, knowing Tonette would trip if she found out, even if she was through with her. Still and all, nothing could keep her from her get-high—especially when she was this close to getting hit off.

"Fuck is wrong with you?" Dame said.

"Don't pay her no mind," said Quita. "She just needs to get right."

"Well," he said, pulling a bag of rocks and a pipe from the pocket of his robe, "she's come to the right place." Both girls' eyes lit up at the sight of the stones, but Dame pulled them back. "Hold on a sec. Let's talk finances. How much y'all got?"

"I don't have any money," Laci said sadly.

"You ain't got no money? Then you ain't got no rock," Dame said, putting the bag back in his pocket.

"Don't act like that," Quita pretended to plead. "We just wanna feel good, daddy."

"Feel good, huh?" Dame smiled.

"Yeah," said Quita. "And if you take care of us, we'll take care of you. Right, Laci?" Laci just stared at the pocket where Dame had put the rocks. "Come on, daddy," Quita added.

"Hmmm," Dame said, scratching his chin. "We're gonna have to work something out here."

"I can pay you back," Laci spoke up. "I'm good for it. My family has money. Tell him, Quita."

"Shorty, I ain't wit' all that. No cash, no stash. But you know what? You a cute lil' bitch, so I'ma have a heart. Y'all get right," he said, tossing the bag on the table. "We'll discuss payment later."

Laci and Quita damn near collided trying to get to the bag. Quita, being the more aggressive of the two, won out. She had first pick of the rocks. Laci just took what was left over. The two girls went to their respective corners and began their routine.

Dame studied Laci's internal battle from a distance and became aroused. Intercourse with Laci would be more than just sex. Dame's ego exploded when he imagined himself conquering her high-yella ass. Despite his success in the illegal drug market, his dark skin had only allowed him to play in a certain league when it came to women. But today would be different.

"Don't get too comfortable with my shit, now, 'cause something got to give," Dame barked. Dame had been ranting for quite a while, but Laci ignored every word that came out of his mouth. She looked around at her surroundings, and she wasn't the least bit bothered by the fact that there were all kinds of drug paraphernalia lying around. All she could think about was getting high at any cost.

I'm doing fine on Cloud Nine . . .

Laci's eyes rolled back in her head as the crack kicked in. Dame's shit was the bomb. It took only seconds before the whole right side of her face and tongue was numb. It didn't take long for her and Quita to smoke up what Dame had given them. Dame had had enough of watching them get high off of his shit. It was time to collect. He dropped his pants where he stood, holding his dick with two hands. He was feeling very confident.

"Yo," he spoke up. "I know y'all bitches wanna get high, but we gots to come to an understanding. I ain't setting out no more rock till we discuss payment. What's up?"

"I . . . I told you I . . . I don't have any money," Laci slurred.

"Lil' bitch," he sneered. "You think I'm holding my dick 'cause I want ya money? Nah, baby, I want it in trade."

"Go see him," Quita said, nudging Laci forward. "And remember what I said. Don't act stupid."

Dame was standing there naked, holding a bag of rocks. His huge penis swung back and forth as he shook the bag. Laci looked at him with disgust. There was no way she was going to do anything with Dame. Yet no sooner than she had the thought, her legs started moving in his direction. As Laci slowly walked toward Dame, Quita started taking off her clothes. Dame told Laci to stop when she was approximately five steps away from him. He wanted her to get on her knees and crawl the rest of the way.

"Get down and crawl," Dame snarled. "Crawl your ass over here."

"What?" Laci asked, thinking that she must have heard him wrong.

"I said crawl," he repeated.

"I will not," she said defiantly.

"Oh, you will," he said, packing a pipe and lighting it. He didn't pull on it. He just let the smoke float into the air. "You'll crawl, or you'll kick ya habit."

Laci thought about the pains that had rocked her body the last time she'd gone without a hit. It was something that she wouldn't wish on anybody. The thought of getting sick and the threat of sobering up made Laci weak. She knew that she would be degrading herself, but the call was so strong. Laci started to bend down, but Dame stopped her.

"I want you to strip first," he said. "Take your clothes off."

"Go ahead," Quita whispered into her ear. "Ain't nobody gonna know."

Before Laci bent down, Quita went over and unbuttoned her shirt and unfastened her pants, sliding them down to her ankles. Her shapely hips and silky thighs made Dame shake his head and grunt in amazement. Never had he seen such creamy and tender flesh. Quita slipped Laci's arms out of her jacket and shirt and pulled her tank top over her head, exposing breasts that looked like they were dying to be fondled. There Laci stood, naked and in need of a serious high.

Quita knew that the combination of crack and sex, especially for beginners, drove users mad, so she loaded the pipe and kept it within Laci's sight.

"C'mon bitch, crawl over here and get this dick." Dame started to dance and shake his ass for the hidden camera.

Laci's insides boiled over with shame as she made her way to Dame. Her knees burned on his rug, but her addiction helped block out the pain. She required what he had. Laci gently gripped Dame's manhood in her right hand as her left one cuddled his balls. Dame couldn't wait to feel the inside of her hot mouth, so he hurried things along, forcing her head to his crotch.

Quita looked on, rubbing her clit. Like Shaunna, she went both ways. She wanted to eat Laci's pussy just as much as Dame did.

As Laci performed the head clinic, Quita lay on her back, slid her face underneath Laci's ass, and began to kiss her other lips. Quita's experienced tongue made Laci push her pussy against Quita's mouth, briefly laying her face on Dame's stomach in enjoyment. This was all new to Laci. The only person who had ever touched her clit until now was herself.

Dame knew what time it was. He reached for the crack pipe and put it into Laci's mouth. Laci took a full-size hit and held it. The mixture of getting eaten out and the inhalation of crack made her pupils disappear in her head. Dame looked into his hidden camera and flexed.

After furnishing Laci with another rush, Dame went around to where Quita was lying and stuck two of his fingers between her legs, moving them in and out of her. She began to moan, and he swapped his fingers for his penis. Quita's moans weren't just a turn-on for Dame; they aroused Laci as well. She began to lick and suck at Quita's nipples. Laci figured that if she worked shit out with her tongue, then she'd protect her virgin pussy.

The sight of Laci getting into it made Dame wanna pop. Even high as a kite, the lil' bitch was still fine. Dame couldn't help himself from finding out what the little peach tasted like. He turned Laci around and started eating her from the back. She tasted like sun-dried peaches on his tongue. He had to have her.

Dame pulled out of Quita and backed Laci up toward his dick. Laci held back. She knew what was about to go down and the fear of the pain set in. She had never even used a tampon before. She couldn't fathom something as big as Dame's dick running up inside of her. But then she thought about the pain of not being high. Laci knew that she had to go with the lesser of the two evils.

Dame proceeded to put his large penis into Laci's tight little vagina, but it ran into a roadblock. Just when she was about to scream, Quita put the pipe back into her mouth. Laci took a deep pull and exhaled as her eyes welled up with tears. Dame proceeded to enter her all the way. She took it all.

Laci's pussy felt like pure magic to Dame. He had only gotten a couple of good strokes in before he had to pause. She was so warm and tight that he almost squirted prematurely. He stroked her slowly at first, and then he began to beast on her. He expected her to cry out, but she didn't. Laci banged her fists on the floor in both pleasure and pain. She started to beg for more—more of what, her mind couldn't decipher. Quita lay on the floor in front of Laci. She spread her legs and pulled Laci's face toward her pussy. But Laci and Dame were more into each other at this point. Quita's head was cut short because Dame's dick had Laci concentrating more on throwing her ass back into him than on how her tongue moved.

"Dame," Quita moaned. "Dame . . ." He plowed on into Laci. "Dame!"

"What, bitch?" he said, not missing a stroke. "Don't you see me working?"

"I know you ain't trippin' off no crackhead pussy. You in love already, nigga, ain't you?" Quita ran her hands all over her naked body. "You know this is the best pussy you ever had."

"What the fuck is you talkin' 'bout, bitch?" Dame said, holding Laci's hips, attempting to beat her precious goods to death. He pushed her knees to her throat. He needed that shit opened wide so that he could drill all the way up into it.

Dame gave Laci another hit as he continued pounding away at her. She came at the same time the smoke hit her lungs. She had no idea if it was Dame's pipe or the crack pipe that caused the eruption in her body. She didn't care. Dame continued to work her insides. The whole time he just kept thinking about how good she felt. He could feel himself getting ready to cum, so he pulled out and let it go all over her back and butt.

Quita rubbed Dame's cum into Laci's skin like it was lotion and sucked the rest out of him herself. When Dame's dick was clear of sperm, he lit a cigarette. It was only halftime and he was building up for another nut.

"You was lovin' that tight pussy, wasn't you?" Quita asked, shooting Dame an evil look.

"Bitch, pussy is pussy," Dame said, blowing smoke in her face. "I don't give a damn about that basehead bitch. I just wanted to beat, that's all. What? You jealous?"

"I brought the bitch here. How the fuck am I gon' be jealous?"

During Dame and Quita's back and forth, Laci lay on the floor enjoying her high and the aftereffect of her orgasm.

"Shit, you actin' like you jealous," he continued.

"Look, I know she look good and it's understandable if you hooked. I kinda think the shit is funny myself. But I'm sure if Dink and them knew how you was actin', they'd be crackin' on you for days. You should've seen yourself." Quita made faces, mimicking Dame's expressions during the sex.

Laci paid no attention to what was being said. She was in her own world, finishing what was left in the pipe. She could've given two shits about what they were arguing about.

"You forget who the fuck you talkin' to?" The volume of Dame's voice warned Quita that she was about to get her head cut back to the white meat. "Bitch, you got amnesia?"

"N-o-o-o, baby," Quita said, massaging Dame's abdomen. She then kissed him on his neck to defuse any potential problems. "You know I love you, daddy."

Laci was sitting on the floor, curled up against the couch. There was a vacant look in her eyes, and her mouth was half open. If it weren't for her chest heaving up and down, she could have been mistaken for dead. Laci was on cloud nine.

Dame looked at his cigarette and glanced at Laci. From the look in his eyes, Quita knew just what time it was. Dame was a cold nigga by nature, and Laci would soon find out what time it was too.

"Laci!" Dame yelled. "Yo, baby girl, you ready for the second half or what?"

Laci kept up the mute act.

Giving Laci the benefit of the doubt, Dame walked over to her and posed the same question. "Hey, girl. I said are you ready for part two?"

There was still no answer from Laci, so Dame pressed his lit cigarette into her bare back. Laci jumped to her feet and tried to reach the burned spot on her back.

"Ouch!" she screamed. "What the fuck you do that for?"

"Your ass is talkin' now, ain't it?" Quita said as she laughed. "You'll be all right. It ain't nothin' a little smoke won't fix, right?"

Dame caressed Laci's breasts, then dropped to his knees and kissed her stomach. He wanted to be a gentleman, but he had to stay strong because Quita had already called him out. If he licked the precious now, there would be nothing that he could say in his defense. The more his tongue circled Laci's belly button, though, the more intense the feeling to lap her juices became.

"Light the shit, Quita," Dame ordered.

Quita loaded and lit the pipe on Dame's command and gave Laci a hit. As Laci pulled from the pipe, she pushed Dame's head between her legs. Much like the crack had Laci, the pussy had Dame. He let her lead him toward her pussy.

Quita looked at her man being humbled in disbelief. He could kick the shit out of her and call her out of her name, but he wanted to be suave with this bitch. She felt repulsed. Quita ground her teeth as her man pleasured Laci the same way he did her. Laci bucked and whined as Dame ate her out.

Quita was red with anger and stomped out of the living room and into the bathroom. She paced back and forth in complete rage. There was no way that bitch was gonna play her out like that. The plan she and Dame had laid down was going to the left. It was time for Quita to make shit right.

Dame got his second wind and pushed back up inside Laci. He was captivated by her beauty and the facial expressions she made as his dick slid in and out of her. He pumped away like a dog in heat while she threw it back like a vet.

Laci opened her eyes and took a good look at Dame. Here was this supposed-to-be-hard drug dealer, soft as Wonder Bread up in the pussy, whining like a bitch. His funny-looking face, coupled with the drug, made Laci giggle. The giggling soon turned into plain laughter.

Dame was trying to get his second nut off when he realized that Laci was laughing at him. He tried to close his eyes and act like he didn't see it, but he could feel her body shaking. Dame paused and looked at her like she was crazy. She was staring right back at him, laughing her ass off. Then suddenly, she realized that he was on to her.

"I'm sorry, baby," she said, rubbing her hands across his chest. "I was just thinking that when you make certain faces, you look like Donkey Kong." She began laughing again.

Dame couldn't believe that another side of him had finally showed itself. It was a side that managed to allow him to please somebody else other than himself. And now here this bitch was laughing at him—a basehead bitch at that. Aiming at Laci's face, Dame drew back and smacked the pipe out of her lips, clear across the room.

Dame began to breathe heavily and then growl. "So you think I'm funny-looking, huh?"

Frightened, Laci quickly pushed herself out from underneath Dame and crawled to the side of the couch for shelter. He grabbed her by her curly ponytail and pulled her back toward him. He forgot all about the camera rolling as he prepared to put Laci's ass to sleep.

Laci observed the fierce look in Dame's eyes. "Quita!" she began yelling. "Quita!"

Dame grabbed her by her chin.

"Get off me," Laci struggled. "Stop! Quita!"

Through the bathroom door, Quita heard the commotion and ran out to see what was happening. Dame had Laci on the floor, trying to knock her head off. The Lord was on Laci's side, because every time Dame tried to connect, he just missed her as she moved her head from side to side, dodging blows.

"Dame?" Quita shouted. "What the fuck you doin'? Leave her alone!"

On one hand, Quita felt good about the ass-kickin'. She'd rather see Dame bust Laci upside the head than give her head. But on the other hand, she was afraid that Dame was going to kill Laci and that she would somehow be blamed for the dead body. Fearing a bid, Quita jumped on his back and tried to calm him down.

Dame bucked, but Quita held fast. He tried to swat her off, but her grip was too tight. Quita didn't want to get into it with Dame, but she feared the worst. Murder was something she wasn't going to sit back and watch go down. She didn't want any part of that, so she maintained her grasp.

Laci held the side of her head and shot a murderous stare at Dame. In all of her seventeen years, a man had never put his hands on her. Besides how to be a backstabbing bitch, there was one thing she had learned from her girls, and that was that turn-about was fair play. Laci used the commotion of Dame trying to remove Quita from his back to get some get-back. She quickly gathered her clothes and what was left of Dame's drugs and slipped out the door.

Dame was heated that the lil' bitch had gotten away with his shit. Ordinarily, he would have arranged for her to be put six feet under, but with a little editing of the tape, he was going to make her a star.

CHAPTER 19

Thinking of a Master Plan

"YO, SOMEBODY PAGE Dink from this number?"

"Nigga, it's Dame," Dame said from the other end.

"I've been lookin' for you for hours," Dink immediately dug into Dame.

"So I heard," Dame said nonchalantly.

"Where the fuck you been?" Dink said with authority.

"Oh, just chillin', nigga," Dame said, dismissing the tone Dink was using with him. "Me and Smurf been fuckin' with some bitches. And we was watchin' this tape of this lil' freak bitch I recorded a couple weeks ago. Man, come to find out, that bitch was a virgin. I'll let you check it out. My man, Play, from Brooklyn is making mad copies for the black market. No charge, either. He said he recognized the ho, she tried to short him, so he's willin' to do that shit on the house. You know, tapes in the hood make more money than at the box office. Bitches better recognize the next time they drop they drawers." Dame released an evil laugh. "Yo, but I just dropped that cat, Smurf, off. Speaking of that little nigga . . . he don't take his strap off for nothin', huh? Homeboy was fuckin' this chick with his gun on. He crazy as hell."

"Nigga," Dink snapped, finally able to get a word in edgewise, "I ain't interested in that shit. We need to discuss how the fuck you've been conducting ya business, partner."

"Fuck is ya problem?" Dame asked, matching his tone. "I told you, I got this over here, man."

"Yeah, just like you had that Titus thing, too. Dame, miss me with that shit. You fucking up, son."

"Dink, how you sound?" Dame asked, offended. "You coming at me like I'm one of them okey-doke soldiers."

"You get what ya hand calls for."

"You bugging, Dink. I don't even like the way you're coming at me. You ain't got no right—"

"I got every right, cousin," Dink cut him off. "I was holding sway and put you down, remember?"

"You talking like I ain't bring nothing to the table, son. How many niggas I rocked for the team?"

"It ain't about that," Dink insisted. "It's about the way you're doing things now. Look, I'm sending some of my people down to help you out. All you gotta do is tell 'em what you need and everything will be cool."

"I don't need no help, yo. I got my own soldiers. We good."

"You know what? I'll take care of everything," Dink declared. "It's my hood. I got it."

"Why you buggin'?" Dame asked defensively.

"Nah, I ain't buggin'," Dink chuckled. "You don't have to do shit."

"What you tryin' to say?"

"I ain't *tryin'* to say shit," Dink said, getting frustrated with going back and forth with Dame. "What I *am* sayin' is that you don't have to do shit, muthafucka!"

Dame was his own man. He was tired of taking orders, especially from an ol' cocky, ego-trippin' nigga. Dink was talking some bullshit and he didn't like it. Dame felt like he was in a position to make things happen without him. "Let me put you on to something, my man," Dame said slyly. "You ain't no-fuckin'-body. Before I came into the fold, niggas was doing whatever the fuck they wanted around here. Now you talkin' 'bout respect the block. *I* brought the fear to this side, yo. My gun ring off! All that bullshit you poppin', you need to slow it up before you find yaself in a bad way. Word to mine, son."

"What?" Dink said, looking at the phone. *I know this nigga ain't trying to threaten me.* "Aiight. We gon' see about this shit." He slammed the phone down.

Dame was playing himself and he needed to be checked. Dink had long let all the little bullshit slide—the hoes, the slick-ass comments, et cetera. Well, now it was time to take action.

Dink immediately paged Smurf from the pay phone, but he put in his car phone number. He needed to put things in order within his camp. He couldn't focus on helping Laci if his own affairs weren't in order. That just wouldn't do.

He had almost forgotten all about the food, so he rushed back into the chicken spot and placed an order. Crystal was switching the dials on the radio when Dink finally got back in the car. He handed her the food without saying a word. She immediately noticed that something was wrong. His body had become rigid and he was flexing his jaw muscle.

"What's the matter, Dink?" she asked with a look of concern.

"Nothing I can't handle," he assured her. "I'm just waiting on a phone call. Did my phone ring?"

"No. Who you waiting on a call from?" Crystal asked. She couldn't help but wonder if he was expecting a call from Laci. Monique said she'd seen Dink driving her around the hood yesterday. "Must be important if it's got you all uptight like this."

"It's just business."

Dink tried to hide his anger, but he knew Crystal picked up on it. He wanted to tell her what was wrong with him and be comforted, but he couldn't put his team at risk, especially his lil' man. Before Dink could think on it further, the car phone rang.

"What's up, D?" Smurf asked from the other end. "Your shit read *9-1-1*. What's poppin'?"

"Ain't nothing," Dink huffed. "Got some shit that I need you to do, though."

"Just give me the basics," Smurf said, paying full attention.

"Ya man," Dink began. "The nigga you was wit' a while ago. You know who I'm talking about?"

"Yeah," Smurf said, smiling and rubbing his dick. Just the thought of puttin' one in Dame gave him a hard-on. "I know just who you mean, son."

"His time is up." The phone sounded as if it had gone dead. "You still there?"

"Yeah, I'm here," Smurf confirmed.

"You heard me?"

"Yeah, I heard."

Smurf and Dame were all right since they had been hanging lately, but they weren't like he and Dink were. They had fucked some bitches and gotten high together, but that shit didn't count for much at the moment. What mattered was that Dink wanted him gone, and he had called on Smurf to do it. The teen knew that Dink had something brewing in his heart, and he would be busy for the next few weeks. Getting the go-ahead to do Dame was cake. But if ever the day came when Dink asked him to do Marco . . . that shit would be the icing.

"Time frame?" Smurf asked.

"Yesterday," Dink replied.

"Aiight. Consider it a done deal. What about his business?"

"That nigga ain't gon' make or break my shit. This has been a long time comin'."

"Yeah, I knew this was gon' happen. I knew that if you weren't makin' plans to take care of him, the business was going to eventually fall apart. That nigga wants to shine more than he wants to grind. He wanted your spotlight, boss. Even God had to eventually throw Satan's ass out the gates."

"Yeah," Dink said with a sigh as he listened to the lil' nigga make sense. "You can only give a nigga a pass but so many times. He asked for it." Dink paused. "I know you two was gettin' kind of cool there for a minute. You got a problem wit' it?"

"It's whatever you say," Smurf said, avoiding the trap. "You my nigga, and I'ma rock wit' you."

"Keep this quiet. I want to tell Marco about this myself. I know that he ain't gon' have no problems with it. He can't stand that nigga. If it wasn't for me, Marco would've tried to fire him on his own."

"I doubt that," Smurf chuckled. "But that's ya man. I'll get wit' ya tomorrow, son." Smurf hung up the phone and went back to reading *The Devil's Tear Drop.* Dame was cool, but Dink was his employer. Smurf wasn't trying to bite the hand that was feeding him. Dame had to go.

Dink hung up the phone and took a deep breath. He hated that it had to go down this way, but fuck it. He figured he was getting ready to start a new life anyhow, so he needed to rework some things. He would eventually sever ties with the streets, but not just yet. Things needed to be put into perspective.

Dink scratched his chin and thought about what he was going to do next. He turned to say something to Crystal and she hopped into his lap. She grabbed Dink by the face and threw her tongue in his mouth. She kissed him long and passionately. He returned her affection, but the thought of killing Dame, cutting her off, and hanging up his hustler's hat made him pull away.

"Crystal, what are you doin'?" He was not in the least interested in her.

"What does it look like I'm doin'? I can see you have a lot on your mind right now. Let me help you forget about some of it. Now stop fighting me, Dink."

"Crystal . . ." Dink said, hesitating.

"Don't fight me, baby," Crystal whispered, kissing him again. "Ain't you tired of fighting?"

"Hold that thought." He looked down at his beeper. "I'll be right back." Dink hopped out of his car and went to use the pay phone. It was Marco. He couldn't wait to reveal his master plan, but there was no way he could have this conversation in front of Crystal.

"Talk to me," Marco said into the phone.

"It's D. You just paged me, man?"

"What up, nigga?"

"Man, what *ain't* up," Dink replied, running his hand down his face. "I got lots of shit to holla at you about."

"Oh, yeah? What it look like?"

"Man, I'm thinking about making some changes."

"Changes like what?" Marco asked.

"First off, I'm 'bout to cut Crystal off."

"Yeah, and?" Marco said, knowing that there was more. Dink took a deep breath.

"And I'm thinking about early retirement, fam."

"Get the fuck outta here!" Marco shouted in disbelief.

"Naw, man. I ain't playing," Dink assured him. "I've been runnin' the streets all my life, son. There's gotta be something better out here for me." Dink had a view of his car from where he stood. He looked through the car window at Crystal, who just happened to be smiling at him. "As a matter of fact, I *know* there's something better out there for me."

"Well, when did all of this shit happen?" Marco said.

"Man, I've been thinkin' about this for a grip now," Dink said. "I just see myself doin' something bigger and better. I can't see me doin' this shit at thirty-five, forty years old. I might want to have a wife and a family someday."

"A wife and family?" Marco gasped. "What kind of shit you smokin'?"

"My head has never been clearer," Dink told him. "I know what I want for my life."

"Man, you sound like a whole different dude. I hope you know what you're doin'. You know what they say about gettin' out of the game, son."

"Yeah, but with a good woman by me, I can do this shit, man."

"But you just said you was 'bout to cut your woman off," Marco reminded him.

"I ain't talkin' 'bout her," Dink said, looking over at Crystal.

"Then who you talkin' 'bout?"

"You don't know her."

"Nigga, I know everybody you know," Marco said, sucking his teeth. "Who is she? Where is she from?"

Dink closed his eyes and took a deep breath. He might as well put it out there. In the hood, the shit was gon' get out there regardless. It might as well come from the horse's mouth.

"Laci. Her name is Laci."

"Laci? Who the fuck is Laci?"

Dink gave a sigh of relief that Marco hadn't heard anything about a Laci on the streets. "I told you that you didn't know her, man, so just let it go."

"Whatever, man."

"You sound upset," Dink teased.

"How long have you known her?" Marco grilled him.

"Long enough," Dink said.

"How long is long enough?" Marco said, not about to let Dink slide with that lame-ass answer.

"I don't know. About a month," Dink answered.

"What? A month? What kind of shit you on, nigga? You ready to give up the game for a girl you ain't known but a month?" Marco was too beside himself. "You playin' yourself, D. You playin' your crew." Marco had his own reasons for not wanting Dink to give up the life and run off with some bitch.

"Nah, Marco, you wrong about that. I think I'm gon' marry this girl."

Marco started laughing out of frustration. "How the fuck you gon' marry somebody you've only known a month, dude? Do that sound smart to you?"

Dink turned his back to Crystal, who he had a feeling was trying her hardest to listen to his conversation. "Yo, I ain't talkin' 'bout gettin' married right away," he whispered. "We gonna establish a relationship and maybe get a place together in Boston or some shit. It'll be a while before I settle down and get married, but I'm gonna do it one day."

"Whatever you're using is what we need to be selling, 'cause it's got you fucked up," Marco laughed.

Dink chuckled. "You crazy, yo."

"No, you the one that's crazy," Marco said. "I know one thing, though. If you leave, me and Dame gon' knock heads like a muthafucka."

Dink grinned. "Well, you ain't gon' have to worry about Dame much longer."

"What you talkin' 'bout?" Marco asked curiously.

"Like I said, you ain't gon' have to worry about that nigga."

"Why? Is he tryin' to run off and get married too?"

"Nah. That nigga's time is up. He's done."

"Well, it's about fuckin' time," Marco said. "You know if it wasn't for you, I would've *been* cancelled the nigga. What made you finally pull the trigger on that fool?"

"He just don't listen," Dink half-lied. "And he's been doin' a lot of shit that he needs to pay for. I don't really want to get into all of that, but he gon' pay."

"Man, if you could see the smile on my face."

"Yeah, I knew you were gon' like to hear that."

"You put Smurf on him?"

"Yeah. He got that covered. And you need to stay away from Dame if you don't want to get caught in the crossfire."

"Bet," Marco said. "But back to this marriage shit. I still feel funny about that."

"Nigga, you act like I'm talking about tomorrow. It ain't like that. I just met somebody I click with. I want all my niggas to meet that special girl in their life one day. Then you'll see what I'm talkin' about."

"Fuck bitches, man," Marco said hatefully. "I ain't fuckin' with them like that."

"Damn, kid. You're the most woman-hating man I've ever met in my life. I should know, my daddy was a pimp." Dink didn't want to press the subject. Marco and women was always a touchy subject. "Don't nothin' feel as good as a warm pussy, nigga."

"Whatever," Marco said, sucking his teeth.

Crystal had had enough of Dink's phone calls. She honked his horn to get him to rush his conversation and get back in the car.

"Yo, let me get out of here," Dink said. "I'll speak to you first thing tomorrow. Better yet, as soon as I hear from Smurf, I'll call you."

CHAPTER 20

Make It Last Forever

DINK LOOKED INTO Laci's eyes and felt sheer passion.

Everything after that seemed to go in slow motion. They both exhaled when their lips touched. They shared a kiss that only soul mates share. Laci massaged the top of Dink's head, and he softly began caressing her breasts.

"Hold on," Dink said, pulling away.

"What?" Laci whined.

"I can't do this, Laci."

"This?" Laci asked, puzzled. "What do you mean *this*?"

"I can't disrespect you like this," he said, looking around. "In a car? No, I won't allow you to go out like that."

"Please allow me to," Laci said, clawing at his pants and trying to kiss him again.

"Goddammit, Laci, no," he said, grabbing her. "You deserve better than some dude fucking you in a car."

"But you're not just some dude, Dink," Laci said, stroking him softly.

"You know what I mean, girl. Regardless of what you've been out here doing, you ain't some whore who drops her panties in the front seat of no man's car, and I'm not going to ever treat you like that. Don't ever allow yourself to be treated like that either."

Dink paused as Laci climbed from his lap and sat back in the passenger seat. Laci had never been with a man who wanted to stop when things got hot and heavy. She knew Dink wanted to fuck her because his dick was rock hard, but he showed restraint out of respect. She knew at this point that what came out of his mouth was legitimate and he meant business.

DURING THEIR DRIVE to Laci's house, they went over their plan. Laci was to tell her mother everything, no matter how hard it was. Dink had explained to her that she needed all the help and support she could get, and that her mother couldn't help her with a problem she didn't know about.

"Damn, this is your house?" Finally, Dink got a chance to see where Laci came from, why she was so different.

"Yeah, I know it's big. We have a gardener and a maid who come help my mother twice a week. I don't know what my mother is going to do with herself once I'm gone."

"How many rooms is it?"

"Five bedrooms, six bathrooms, two living rooms, and a pool in the back," Laci spouted off, unfazed by her plush lifestyle. The white brick Colonial-inspired home had four pillars in front, similar to the White House. In all his years of stackin' chip, Dink had never seen a home like this. Of course he'd imagined it and if he wanted to, he could drop the cash right now and buy the home that was for sale right across the street. However, until he met Laci he'd had no real desire to leave the hood. Actually, he'd never thought he could.

Focusing back on the matter at hand, Dink checked himself and turned to Laci. "Now page me if you need me, girl. Aiight?" He looked directly into her eyes. She cracked a smile. "What?"

"Nothing. It just feels like I've been with you all my life. You know how it is in the movies? You get to see someone's entire life in ninety minutes. Well, that's how this day has felt."

Dink smiled back at her. "Well, you definitely gon' get more than ninety minutes out of me, girl. But like I was saying, hit me up anytime during the night. I got some business I need to take care of in the morning, then I'm going to come back through to check you out. Is that cool?"

Laci nodded. Dink wanted to get up first thing in the morning and get some info on rehabs so that he didn't show up empty-handed. He promised Laci he would help her and that's exactly what he planned on doing. From here on out, any obstacle facing either one of them they'd tackle together.

Dink made sure Laci understood how serious he was about her kickin' that shit. He told her that he intended to go as far as patting her ass down if necessary. If they were going to try and do the damn thang, she had to get her shit back in order. And college still had to be part of her future. If it were up to Dink, she'd start on time with the rest of the freshmen.

Dink warned Laci to stay away from the Jackson Projects, too. And he told her that if she really wanted help, then she would have to help herself as well. He wasn't going to try to pull dead weight.

"I know all this might sound like I'm just trying to step up in your life and take over, but this is what I gotta do. Do you understand that?"

"Yes, I do," Laci said like an obedient child.

"Then you have to put all of your energy into leavin' this crack shit alone. You ain't been on it that long, so maybe that counts for something. Right now your mind is just caught up in it. It's got you thinking your body needs it, but it don't. It ain't gonna be easy, but we'll get through it. Are you with me?"

"Sure, Dink," Laci said, trying to sound confident.

"Well, I'm gon' head out."

"Dink?" Laci said softy.

"Yeah."

"Where you headed? To Crystal's?" Laci couldn't help but ask.

Dink sighed. "Don't even think like that. I'm takin' care of her. She's gon' get what she's got comin' to her. Don't worry about it. You have my word on that. So, are you truly with me?"

Laci paused. Life with Dink would be a gamble. She could try and make it work with him, but what if he turned out to be just like everybody else who'd tried to befriend her? Looking at her other options, which were somewhere between very few and none, Laci was willing to take a chance.

"Yes, of course I'm with you."

"Good. Now head on in that house and handle your business with your moms."

"Okay," Laci said. She leaned in, kissed Dink good night, and opened the car door. Before getting out she turned toward him.

"Don't hurt me," Laci said with desperate eyes. "Please don't hurt me, Dink."

"I'll never hurt you. We're going to grow old together and sit on our porch drinkin' lemonade, watchin' our grandkids play."

Laci put her head down and smiled. "Do you promise?"

Dink looked at her warmly. There was nothing he wanted to do more at this moment than just take her in his arms and ride away somewhere far—to get away from all the bullshit forever. But right now he couldn't offer her that. Right now all he could offer her was his word. "I promise."

CHAPTER 21

Too Little, Too Late

LACI WOKE UP the next day thinking that the night before was all a dream. That was until the grip showed up twice as strong. The desire to smoke wasn't the only thing that had her wide awake. The phone kept ringing. Her mother must have already gotten up and headed out for the day or else she would have answered it by now. Laci tried to sleep through the annoying rings, but her craving wouldn't let her rest.

The night before, Dink had occupied her time and thoughts. He had been her rock. But now, all she had was a craving for that get-high.

"Hello," Laci said, frustrated with the caller.

"Hello? Can I speak to Laci?" the caller asked.

"This is she," Laci said, clearing her throat.

There was a pause. "Laci, it's Shaunna." Shaunna figured that two in the afternoon was enough time for anyone to have gotten a sufficient amount of sleep.

"Shaunna?" Laci said, sounding both irritated and surprised.

"Yeah. Where you been, girl? Your mother didn't tell you that I called? I haven't seen or heard from you in weeks."

Laci remained silent, trying to focus her eyes. Hell, it might have been two in the afternoon, but it felt like the middle of the night for her.

"I know that you haven't heard from me in a while, but I did try to call you."

"What do you want?" Laci asked dryly. She wasn't interested in anything Shaunna had to say.

"What do I want?" Shaunna asked, as if she was surprised by the response.

"Yeah, you heard me," Laci snapped. "I know you're not my friend. Only *friends* call each other just to say hey. So why are *you* calling me? You feel guilty?"

"Guilty?"

"Yeah, guilty. Why are you trying to act stupid? You were a part of the whole thing too."

"I didn't want to do it, Laci, I swear," Shaunna confessed. "I even got into an argument with the girls after the fact."

"Yeah, whatever, Shaunna. You're just trying to clear your conscience. You don't give a fuck about what happens to me."

"You're wrong, Laci," Shaunna said in a sincere tone.

"The only thing I was wrong about was fuckin' with you and your weak-ass crew."

"I understand that, but I'm tryin' to apologize for my part."

"I don't want an apology from you. What the fuck is an apology gonna do for me now?" Laci sobbed. "What you did to my life . . . oh, man . . . there aren't any words. But I'm not gon' let y'all bitches break me. I'm gon' clean myself up and go off to college as planned. Just watch and see."

"That's good," Shaunna said, genuinely happy for her. "I know you ain't tryin' to hear it, but all I can do is tell you that I'm sorry. I realize I was wrong, and I wouldn't wish on anyone what we did to you."

"You're right. I ain't trying to hear it. But you know what? You can hear my friend Tone." Laci slammed the phone down.

Ring... Ring... Ring...

"Hello!"

"Laci?" asked another familiar voice.

"Quita?" Laci said, shocked to hear her voice on the other end. Nobody had ever given two shits about her before.

"Laci, you know I've been tryin' to get in contact with you forever? What's up? Where have you been?"

Laci began to laugh. "What is it with you bitches, all of a sudden coming out of the woodwork trying to get at me?"

"Damn," Quita said in a stink-ass voice. "Why you trippin'?"

"Why am I trippin'!" Laci exclaimed. "Bitch, you gave me crack! For the past few weeks my life has been fucked up. And instead of helping the situation, you fed me more of the poison. I shouldn't even have to go into what happened at your man's house. As you all say, you violated big time."

"Laci, you came to me," Quita said. "What did you *think* we were going to do—go shopping, do lunch and a movie? I know you mad about everything, but—"

"Mad?" Laci interrupted. "Quita, you tried to kill me."

"Bitch, I saved your life," Quita snapped before catching herself and calming down. "Look, Laci, you being extreme. It wasn't that serious."

"It wasn't that serious?" Laci huffed. "I was a *virgin*, Quita. If I ever have kids one day and just happen to have a daughter, what am I supposed to tell her about my first time? How am I supposed to sit down and have the talk with my daughter, knowing how something so precious was taken from me?"

Quita had no comment.

"Nothing to say, huh?" Laci said. "I'm not going to lie. I wanted to see you dead. But that ain't my place. Besides, you're already half-dead. Good-bye, Quita."

Laci slammed her phone down as hard as she could. After a few seconds passed, it rang again.

"What the fuck!" Laci screamed. Thinking it was Quita calling her right back, she quickly picked up the phone, fully enraged.

"What the fuck do you want now?" Laci shouted into the phone.

"Damn, what did I do?" the caller asked.

"Who is this?" Laci said to yet another female voice on the other end of her phone.

"Laci, it's Monique," Monique said, surprised that Laci was even home. "Where have you been? We've been worried sick."

"What, did all of y'all have a meeting and decide to call me today? This shit is suspect."

"What are you talking about?" Monique asked, confused. "I'm just callin' to see if you're all right. And I can't even lie, you been heavy on my mind."

"Please," Laci said, sucking her teeth. "Guilt has gotten to you, too, huh?"

"Laci, what are you talking about?" Monique played stupid. "What's wrong with you?"

"What's wrong with me? How about that fuckin' crack y'all had me smoke? Does that sound about right?"

"Aw, girl, that was just a joke. It wasn't nothin' serious." Monique giggled nervously.

Laci growled in frustration. If only they knew what she was going through. If only they knew the battle between her brain and her body.

"Why does everybody keep saying the same thing? 'Oh, Laci, it's nothing serious.' I'd hate to see what y'all consider serious." *Click.* Laci hung up again.

MONIQUE'S HEAD WAS still throbbing from the verbal lashing Laci had just laid on her when her phone rang. "H . . . Hello?"

"What you doin', girl?" the caller asked.

"Who is this—Crystal?" Monique asked.

"Yeah, bitch!" Crystal snapped. "Who the hell else it gon' be?"

"What up, girl? I ain't doing nothing—I just finished talking to Laci."

"What the fuck you talkin' to her ass for? Are you crazy? I hope you hung up on that bitch."

"Relax. I was just checkin' on her since we hadn't heard from her in a while."

"Fuck that," Crystal said, becoming more hype.

"Crystal, you not the least bit sorry about what we did?"

"She had it coming, and I'd do the shit all over again if I could. Only this time, I'd make sure the bitch OD'd."

Monique could tell that some shit must have gone down to put Crystal on the rampage.

"What's up?" Monique asked with concern. "What happened?"

"That bitch and Dink rode around all day yesterday like they were the fuckin' Dukes of Hazzard."

"What?" Monique said, shocked.

"Hell, yeah. That's two times now. The bitch is getting real comfortable."

"Hmmm. Dink know Laci out there like that. She had to be trying to cop. He ain't gon' fuck up what y'all have for no crack-head. Then again, he was pushing up hard on her that day at your house. But she wasn't showin' him no kinda love. That was all on your man."

"What?" Crystal got defensive. In her mind, Laci was at fault. She knew Dink would never play her like that.

"I'm just tellin' you what I saw."

"Whatever, Monique. Listen, I'm tired of this sometimey shit. I'm with Tonette now. Either y'all bitches rollin' wit' us or not. And if you rollin' wit us, then you ain't in contact with her. Feel me?"

"Yeah," Monique said in a whisper.

"So, you know what you gotta do then, right?"

"Yeah. I know what I gotta do."

CHAPTER 22

Truth Hurts

MARGARET GOT HOME around three o'clock. By now Laci was fully awake, but not fully functioning. The phone had fucked up her rest with its ringing off the hook. The fucked-up part about it was that not one of the callers was Dink. Perhaps last night *was* just a dream.

Laci heard her mother enter the house. She took a deep breath and braced for the blow. She knew it would be only a matter of minutes before she'd come up to her room and begin her usual interrogation. Laci had succeeded in brushing her mother off, but this time she knew she had to come clean. She had promised Dink that she would. Still, she reconsidered telling her mother everything about a thousand times as she lay in bed, waiting for her to come and check on her. Fuck what she promised Dink. He promised that he would call and he hadn't. Besides, her body still wanted to get high. And if she told her mother, it would only make it more difficult to score and get what she needed.

Several minutes had gone by, and her mother didn't come knocking at her door as expected. Perhaps she had already given up on her before she even asked to be saved.

Laci managed to go to the bathroom and make herself look half presentable. She threw on her favorite Troop jogging suit, which she'd forgotten she even had. She hadn't been the least bit concerned about making a fashion statement lately. Laci stopped in front of the full-length, freestanding mirror beside her closet door. She looked at her reflection for a few seconds until she couldn't stand the sight of herself. Her clear skin was becoming blotchy, her hair had lost its luster, and her eyes and teeth had a yellowish tint. She flipped the mirror so that it was facing the wall. Laci told herself that it would remain in that position until she changed and made herself worth looking at again. She exited her bedroom and began to search for her mother.

"Ma," Laci called as she pushed her parents' bedroom door open. She stuck her head in, but her mother wasn't there. She then proceeded downstairs. "Ma," Laci called again as she entered the kitchen. Still she got no answer. She knew damn well that she had heard her mother come in the house. She had to be there somewhere. Why hadn't she come upstairs to check on her? Why wasn't she answering her call?

Laci proceeded to the living room. When she got there she stopped in her tracks. "Ma," she said in a confused tone. "Ma, what's wrong?"

Sitting on the couch, Margaret's face was flushed. She didn't respond to Laci. She didn't move. She didn't even look up at her.

"Ma, are you okay?" Laci said, slowly walking over to her mother. When she approached, she noticed an envelope and some pictures lying facedown on the couch next to her. There were also a couple of pictures in her hand. "Ma, talk to me. What do you have here?"

"You left me no choice, Laci," Margaret said in a faint voice. "I tried to talk to you. That's what I told him. I said 'I tried to talk to my baby, but she wouldn't be honest and tell me what was going on.' " Margaret's eyes began to well up with tears.

"Who, Mommy?" Laci asked, sitting down next to her. She took the pictures from her hand, looked at them, and turned pale as a ghost.

"Detective Logan," Margaret said. "That's what I told the private eye I hired to see what was going on with you." She finally looked up at Laci. Once Sonny was able to provide her with more info, he'd warned her not to take to the street herself and suggested she hire a professional.

Laci couldn't even look her mother in the eye. She covered her mouth with her hand as tears began falling down her cheeks. She began to sniff and snort, as she couldn't hold back the pain of what she saw in those pictures. It wasn't the fact that they revealed her copping crack, smoking crack, even giving head in parked cars for crack, it was the fact that her mother had seen them.

Laci began to wail as if she were in severe pain. Margaret was too done to even hold her daughter. She was all cried out. All she could do was sit there and face reality.

Laci managed to speak through all of her agony. "This girl doesn't even look like me. That detective played you, Mom."

CHAPTER 23

A Lover Scorned

DINK WAS PLEASED with the way things were going.

Smurf was gonna dust Dame and Marco could take over his territory. Soon he would leave the business to Smurf and Marco. Them niggas couldn't fuck it up too bad. Since he was on a roll at handling shit on his "to do" list, Dink decided to call up his soon-to-be ex.

Crystal's phone rang twice before her answering machine picked up. Dink hated to leave her a message, but he didn't have time to keep trying to get at her to say the simple shit he needed to say.

"Uh, Crystal. It's me," Dink said.

"Hello," Crystal said, out of breath. "Dink?"

"Yeah, what you doin'?"

"I was in the bathroom. Where you been? I see less and less of you these days."

"Yeah, you know how things are. I'm busy as hell. If I don't make the money, someone else will."

"I hear that. Speakin' of money, I need some. When do you think you'll be able to stop by?"

"I don't know."

"How about tonight?" Crystal suggested.

"I don't think that's gon' happen. I got a lot of shit I need to do. Maybe tomorrow. As a matter of fact, I'll see you tomorrow. I'll call you as soon as I can make a move."

Dink could see Crystal's pout through the phone.

"All right," Crystal whispered.

"What's the matter?" he asked.

"I just want to see you. It almost seems like you don't want to be with me anymore. You don't want to be with me, Dink?"

"Never mind, Crystal. I'll just talk to you tomorrow." Dink couldn't bring himself to tell her over the phone. He thought a face-to-face might be in order. That way he could give her an opportunity to explain herself.

"I just miss you, Dink," Crystal said, meaning every word of it.

"Yeah, I know."

"You know?" Crystal said with a faint chuckle. "No, Dink, I don't think you do."

"Yes, I do. Believe me, I do. Like I said, you'll see me, trust me. How are your girls?" Dink fished.

"They all right." Crystal played into it.

"What about the ol' girl with the baby? What's her name?" he asked.

"Shaunna?"

"Yeah, Shaunna. How's she doin'?"

"She cool," Crystal said nonchalantly.

"That's good. What about Dame's girl, Tonette?" Dink said, working his way down the list.

"She crazy, but she aiight," Crystal said, allowing him to carry the conversation.

"What about the college girl?" Dink asked, finally getting to the point.

"Who, Laci? I haven't heard from her," she lied.

"Seriously? Why?" Dink asked, giving Crystal the opportunity to tell him the truth.

"She's a stuck-up, bitch. That's why," Crystal said, sucking her teeth.

"I thought that was your girl."

"Hell, no!" Crystal said without hesitation.

"Why you say it like that?" Dink said, still fishing.

" 'Cause stuck-up bitches make me sick. Laci's a stuck-up bitch, so she made me sick," Crystal said with pure hatred in her voice.

"You sound like you have a personal problem with her."

"She was the kind of girl who bragged about what she had, tryin' to make the rest of us feel bad. We just got sick of her shit and got even. That's all."

"Got even?" Dink inquired, getting angrier and angrier with each word Crystal spoke.

"That's right," Crystal said, not feeling the way he seemed to be so interested in Laci.

"How?" he asked.

"I don't want to talk about it," Crystal said, deliberately leaving Dink on the edge of his seat.

"What? Tell me what you did, Crystal!" he demanded, no longer able to hide his emotions.

"Damn, why you gettin' all mad and shit?"

"You know I don't like it when you start that I-don't-wanna-talk-about-it shit, Crystal."

"Fuck it then," Crystal said, ready to get a rise out of Dink. "We hated her conceited ass, thinking she was smoking weed, when her dumb ass was really smoking crack," Crystal blurted out.

Dink was silent. He didn't think Laci was lying about how she started smoking, but to hear the story come out of Crystal's own mouth made any thoughts of empathy for her go out the window.

"Now I hear that bitch is a strawberry," Crystal laughed. "You wouldn't believe some of the nasty-ass niggas she done let run up in her for a hit of that pipe. You wouldn't believe some of the nasty shit that bitch has done. She'll never get a man now. Her rep is tainted. Anybody would be stupid to fuck with her."

Crystal felt good twisting the knife into the pit of Dink's stomach. If he *was* thinking about fucking with Laci, she hoped she had just made him reconsider.

Dink allowed his anger to boil and continued his conversation with Crystal.

"You gave her crack?" Dink asked. "What kind of shit is that? Where the fuck did you get crack from?"

"Tonette got it from Dame," Crystal giggled.

"From Dame! He gave her crack for that shit y'all pulled?"

"He didn't give it to her. She snuck it from his stash."

"What?" Dink said. When one of the links in Dink's chain was weak, it burned him like gonorrhea. If Tonette could take Dame's shit from right up under his nose, then anyone could.

"Yeah. That's how we got the crack. We got it from Tonette, and Tonette got it from Dame."

"You a cold-blooded bitch," Dink spat. "To do the shit you did, you can't possibly have a heart. You also put all of your cronies in danger."

"What? How?" Crystal said as a stroke of fear brushed over her.

"Laci could press charges on y'all. Did you ever think of that?"

"What are you flappin' about?" Crystal tried to brush it off.

"You do know that crack is illegal?"

"So is weed," Crystal said, like she was telling Dink something new. "Laci ain't gonna say nothin' 'cause them muthafuckas is gonna know she was trying to get high regardless."

"You crazy," Dink said. "Let me paint a picture for you, Crystal. Let's say Laci's mother catches on that her daughter's got the itch and decides to get the authorities involved. They're gonna wanna know where she got the crack, and she's gonna point out all y'all stupid bitches," Dink said in an attempt to scare Crystal. "Then the police will come after y'all, and of course y'all will break. But it doesn't stop there," he continued. "They'd go after Dame, which would fuck up my money. You see how your little bullshit act of jealousy had the potential of fuckin' me?"

The cat had Crystal's tongue.

"You see where I'm going with this?" he asked. "You always do dumb shit that can come back to bite me!"

"I'm sorry," Crystal cried. She had forgotten about her initial intention—to steer Dink away from Laci. "I didn't know that it could hurt you. Please believe that I wouldn't have done it if I knew that it would."

"I don't know, Crystal," Dink continued, sounding like he was her father. "Every time I turn around, there's something new with your ass."

"C'mon, baby. You know I'd never do anything to hurt you. I'll make it up to you. I promise!"

"Make it up to me? How you gon' do that?" Dink asked. "And

I don't know if I can trust you anymore. That was some stupid-ass shit y'all did."

"Don't act like that, daddy," she pleaded.

"I don't know," he sighed.

"Please, Dink. Give me one more chance."

Dink paused as if he was deep in thought before replying. "All right, all right. I may have something that you can do to make it up to me."

"Just name it, Dink," Crystal said desperately.

"I might need you to make a delivery."

"Is that all, daddy?" Crystal said, happy to do it. "Consider it done already."

"I shouldn't even be talking to your ass, let alone giving you a job. But we just gon' start off with something small till I'm sure I can trust you."

"Aiight, well, I'll be able to do that with my eyes closed," Crystal assured him.

"We'll see," Dink said. "Page me first thing in the morning so I can tell you everything you need to know."

"Yes, Dink," Crystal said, eager to please her man.

"Peace."

"I love you, baby," Crystal said, but Dink had already hung up the phone.

He had ended his call with Crystal, but he wasn't finished with her by far. Now he was certain that cutting her off on the phone would even be too good for her. She deserved more than that. Oh, hell, yeah. She deserved much more indeed.

CHAPTER 24

Unfinished Business

SMURF HADN'T KNOWN Dame long, but he knew his style. He had arranged for some fresh-faced PYT named Tammi to get at him. He knew exactly how Dame fell prey to new pussy. That nigga would be all over her, trying to play the cool-ass pimp role. And Smurf was absolutely correct in his assumption, because it wasn't long before Dame began to front and offer to take Tammi into the city. He had a night of dinner and a little fun at an expensive hotel in mind. Tammi agreed, as she had planned to. She would get Dame drunk and then make her move.

Tammi was a fine, yellow chick from Yonkers. She was about 5′9″ and built like a stallion. Tammi was a girl that Smurf knew from going to the strip clubs. And she was a bitch that was always down to get money.

During their bar-hopping, Tammi noticed that Dame was carrying a huge knot of money. He kept flashing it, hoping that it would impress her enough to give him some pussy, but all it really did was motivate her to complete what she'd been hired to do. After bar-hopping, the two ate dinner and headed for the Marriott.

SMURF STROLLED THE streets of Manhattan trying to kill time. It would be a while before Tammi paged him. He had heard that The Village always held an assortment of females, so he headed down that way.

The West Village was like nothing Smurf had ever experienced. It was colorful and wide open. Same-sex couples walked the streets holding hands and kissing. It repulsed Smurf to see such displays of homosexuality. That was something his mother had always taught him was a sin. But then again, who was she to judge anybody? He blocked her from his mind and kept it moving.

Smurf was cutting across a back street when he thought he saw a familiar car in an alley. As he looked more closely, he confirmed that it was Marco's. He wondered what his fat ass was doing in this neck of the woods. He was just about to approach Marco's car when an unmarked Lumina pulled up behind it. The car didn't bear the markings, but Smurf knew pig when he smelled it. He just lay in the cut and watched.

The cop car flicked its high beams twice, then killed the lights. Marco got out of his car holding an envelope. He walked over to the Lumina and climbed into the front. Smurf's mind began to spin. Smurf scratched his head, trying to figure out what the hell was going on. The only time a nigga was supposed to get into a police car was if he was under arrest. Even then, his ass was supposed to get into the backseat. Marco had to be a snitch, just as Smurf had suspected all along. He knew there was something shady about that nigga. Smurf knew that making his move would be dangerous, but fuck it. He lived a dangerous life. As Marco and the officer conversed, Smurf moved in closer.

Inside the car, the unthinkable was going on. Marco handed the officer the dossier containing information on Dink and his drug operations. He didn't like what he was doing, but the police had him by the balls. Dink had told him time and again about riding dirty, but he was a know-it-all. He knew everything except what to tell the police when he got caught with two ounces of coke. Hence, his predicament. He had sacrificed his lifelong friend to save his own skin.

"Is this everything?" the officer asked.

"Yep," Marco said. "Account numbers and how much he clocked this month. It's all there. Can I go now?"

"Not just yet," the officer said with a mischievous look in his eye. "Where are your manners? You haven't even greeted me properly."

"My bad," Marco said. He leaned in, kissing the officer on the lips.

"That's better," the officer said, unbuckling his belt. "Now hook me up before you go."

Marco smiled wickedly as he went down on the officer.

Smurf watched as Marco leaned over into the officer's lap. The officer threw his head back in ecstasy as Marco's head bobbed up and down.

If Dink could see him now, he would shit a brick. Marco was down-low faggot. Molested as a child and raped in prison before coming to terms with his sexuality, Marco harbored his feelings for men until he was able to unleash them, far, far away from his boys. But the biggest secret of all that determined whether Marco lived or died was his love for Dink—not brotherly love, but love-love. Needless to say, the thought of Dink falling for some chick and going away with her didn't sit well with him at all.

It took all of Smurf's self-control to keep him from emptying his gun into the Lumina's windshield. It was bad enough that Marco was dealing from the bottom, but he was a homo, too! That shit was crazy. Dink had been good to all of them. He'd made them a family, and that muthafucka Marco had turned out to be rotten.

Smurf wanted to call Dink and tell him what was up. He wanted Dink to give him the go-ahead to blast that nigga on the spot. But he knew Dink all too well. He would have wanted Smurf to fall back and let him handle things himself. Smurf couldn't see walking away from the scene before him, so he made a judgment call. He disappeared into the shadows and waited.

WHEN IT CAME to sex, Dame enjoyed being aggressive. He had never met a female that was confident enough to flip the script, but there was a first time for everything. Tammi loved sex and being in control. She was a vet and extremely conscious of how the thought of sex made all men, at some point, fall victim. But right now she had a job to do and intended on keeping it street.

From the moment they walked through the door of their hotel room, Tammi took charge. She wouldn't let Dame touch her unless she gave him permission. Dame was thrown off balance. He was a man who liked being in control. He wasn't used to a female taking the lead. Normally he would have been pissed off, but strangely enough, he was turned on by it.

"Turn your ass around, nigga!" Tammi commanded. Dame reached out to feel her breasts, but she wanted her ass felt. "Feel this ass, nigga," she said as she grabbed his hand.

"What the fuck you doing?" Dame said, jerking his hand away.

"Nothin', baby. You scared of me?" she purred. "You afraid of a woman that takes the lead?"

"Shit!" Dame stepped back toward Tammi, attempting to seduce her with his kisses. Tammi still wanted her way, and she grabbed his hands and placed them on her ripe ass.

"Here, you feel that?" she asked. "Doesn't it make your dick hard?"

Dame figured he'd play Tammi's game, just as long as intercourse was at the end of the tunnel.

"Yeah, ya shit is crazy soft. Damn, girl. You got my ear. I'm listenin' like a muthafucka."

Tammi unbuttoned Dame's pants and pulled out his penis. She was impressed, but this was business, not pleasure. She put his dick in her mouth and began to blow him.

"Damn, baby," he moaned.

"You like that?" she asked, looking up at him. "Tell me you like that." She continued to suck.

"I like it," he groaned. "Yeah, baby. Do that shit."

Dame closed his eyes and tilted his head back as Tammi pleasured him. He was so into it that he never saw her slide the switchblade from the tote she was carrying. Tammi worked Dame's dick with one hand and opened the knife with the other. She took her mouth off of him and with a sweep of her arm, she cut his dick completely off. Dame tried to scream as he leaned over in pain, but Tammi was quick to cut his throat.

As Dame lay there dying, Tammi relieved him of all his goods. All his jewelry and every dime in his pocket went into her tote. As the life escaped his body, his anger grew; however, he had no choice but to lie there, helpless. Dame had hated and abused women all his life, only to have karma catch up with him. It was a woman who brought him into the world and a woman who took him out.

Tammi checked herself one last time in the mirror to make sure she looked okay. Everything was straight. She glanced at Dame. "You were a big one, too. Too bad, baby. I'll bet you could fuck the shit out of a bitch, huh?" She blew him a kiss and exited the room.

Once Tammi had left the hotel building, she walked a couple of blocks and hailed a taxi. In addition to nice jewelry, she had a total of twelve thousand dollars in her tote. She would report five to Smurf and cuff the seven. Hell, she had to eat too. After giving the driver instructions on where to take her, she settled into the backseat to enjoy the ride.

SMURF WAITED NEARLY a half-hour for Marco to get out of the Lumina and for the officer to drive off. Finally, Marco was in the alley alone. When the officer's car was out of sight, Smurf slid up behind Marco as he was getting back into his car.

"Yo!" Smurf said.

"What the fuck!" Marco jumped. "You scared me, kid."

"My bad," Smurf said with his arms folded. "I was walking by and I saw your car. What you doing down this way, fam?"

"Minding my business, lil' nigga." Marco didn't like Smurf's demeanor. "Fuck you doing questioning me?"

"Nah," Smurf said, moving a little closer to Marco. "Seeing your car parked here in this dark-ass alley down in The Village just seemed a little funny, that's all. I mean, I know *we* ain't got no business down here."

Marco could have kicked himself for not strapping his pistol.

He had taken it off and put it in his glove box before meeting up with the officer. He knew Smurf's M.O. If he dared reach for it, Smurf would surely kill him. He had to play it cool and see what the kid knew.

"Ain't nothing. I was down here wit' a bitch," Marco lied.

"Where she at?" Smurf asked, looking around.

"Uh . . . around the corner using the bathroom. She should be done by now, so let me pull the car around to meet her."

"I'll ride with you," Smurf volunteered, getting in the passenger's side. Smurf picked up Marco's car phone and started dialing

"Who you calling?" Marco jumped in the driver's seat.

"Naw, nobody, forget it." Smurf said, putting the phone down carefully so that it didn't hang up.

"I mean . . . come on. Why you wanna be a third wheel?"

"Same reason you wanna be a snitch!" said Smurf, unfolding his arms and exposing the Glock he had been concealing in his right hand. "I seen the whole thing, Marco. As good as Dink was to you, why?"

Marco just sat there staring at Smurf. Then something came to mind. If Smurf saw him in the car with the officer, then nine times out of ten he saw *everything*. First it was Dame who had caught Marco with a man almost in that very same spot. He'd lied his way out of it, telling Dame that he didn't see what he thought he had seen, but Dame knew better. Marco wasn't totally certain that Dame truly believed him. And with no words at all, Dame held that incident over his head. Finding out that Dame's lights were getting put out had lifted a huge weight off Marco's shoulders. As the saying goes: when one door closes, another one opens. He supposed that Smurf was that new open door.

Marco knew that there was no way out this time. He knew

what his destiny was with this lil' nigga. No need being a punk now. "Fuck you, lil' nigga," Marco spat. "I did what I had to do. It was me or Dink, fam. That's the way shit is out here—survival of the fittest. A lot of shit you wouldn't understand, son."

"You know what? I might not understand a lot of shit, but I understand loyalty." Smurf fired two shots into Marco's heart. He raised the car phone to his ear. "You hear all that, Dink?"

"Yeah," Dink replied from the other end. "I heard it all."

DINK SAT IN his car as a lone tear ran down his cheek. When his car phone had rung minutes earlier, he'd picked it up to say hello but didn't hear anything. Then he heard what sounded like Smurf and Marco having an argument. As he listened in, he understood what was going down. Marco was a snitch.

He and Marco had grown up together. When Marco got locked up, Dink took care of him. When he came home, Dink put him on. Marco had rewarded Dink's kindness with treachery. He wiped his eyes and tried to gather his wits. He would miss the Marco he thought he knew, but that was how the game went.

Dink hung the car phone up and pulled up to the most beautiful house on the street, knocked on the front door twice, and waited. After a few moments, a woman came to the door and eyed him suspiciously. He knew she had to be Laci's mother—they looked so much alike.

"Mrs. Johnson," Dink spoke in a clear voice. "My name is Din—I mean Daryl. I'm here to talk to you about Laci."

TAMMI PAGED SMURF as soon as she got out of the cab. It took him about five minutes to walk to where she was on West Eighth Street. When he spotted her standing in front of the train station, she didn't even looked nervous. Tammi had just caught a body, but she was calm and collected. Smurf almost felt sorry for what he was about to do to her.

"Hey, baby," she said with a smile.

"Did you take care of business?" Smurf cut to the point.

"Of course I did. Shit. I told you that it was a piece of cake. That nigga was easy. All I had to do was give him some head and it was a wrap."

"Whatever. Did you get any money from him?"

"A little something. Not much," she lied.

"What's 'not much'?" he questioned.

"A couple grand or so."

"A couple grand?" Smurf asked in disbelief. Dame was a baller. That nigga was a pimp. Smurf knew he had to be holding more than that. "You sure? That nigga Dame wouldn't be caught dead with less than five grand in his pocket."

"I beg to differ," Tammi said with a devilish grin. "But seriously, that's all he had. I was just as surprised as you. I thought that I was gon' have a grip, and all I ended up with was a pinch."

"I hear you," Smurf said, sizing her up. "Don't worry about it. You keep that for your trouble. Come on so I can give you the rest of your money." Smurf walked down a side street. Tammi followed behind.

"You giving it to me now?" she asked. "Niggas usually have this twenty-four-hour waiting period so they can confirm the shit."

"Yeah?" Smurf said. "Would you rather get it tomorrow?"

"No!" she said greedily, running behind him.

"What you been up to lately?" he asked, making small talk.

"On the grind," she responded. "Stripping ain't paying like it used to. Niggas is getting cheaper by the day."

"I hear that, ma. Yo, let me ask you something. Was you born stupid or did you have to work on it?"

Tammi was still pondering the question when Smurf hit her with the Glock. He fired two bullets into her chest, monkey-flipping her to the concrete. He dug through her tote and found the twelve grand she was trying to cuff. Smurf took off his jacket and wrapped it around the tote. He then placed it under his arm and got off the block. *Damn, I'm hungry, all this work got a nigga starving,* he thought.

CHAPTER 25

What You Won't Do for Love

DINK, MARGARET, UNCLE Sonny, and Laci all sat around the coffee table. Margaret and Laci's eyes were worn and red from crying. Everything that Laci had gone through had finally been laid on the table—the drugs, the sex, everything. Laci painted a much more descriptive picture than the private eye's snapshots could ever have portrayed. Margaret almost fainted twice, but Uncle Sonny managed to revive her.

Margaret was amazed at Dink's courage and honesty. He told her about his sordid past, his career choice, and his plan to retire so he could be there for Laci. Margaret was a little thrown by him at first, but she respected his strength. She could tell by looking in his eyes that he really cared for her daughter. Most young men didn't even take the time to come and meet a girl's parents. Here, Dink was demanding an encounter.

The four of them discussed the best way to handle Laci's recovery. Margaret and Uncle Sonny knew of a few programs out of state. Finally, they found one that sounded like it had the perfect twelve-step program for Laci. It was also the only one that had a bed available, but it was all the way in North Carolina. While she was in rehab, her mother would tell everyone she was vacationing in Puerto Rico. Margaret hated the thought of sending her daughter away, but she needed help. Dink promised Margaret that he would make sure Laci got to the facility safely, and he would fly back and forth to check on her as much as possible.

While Margaret, Uncle Sonny, and Dink took care of business, Laci went to her room to rest. She curled up in a fetal position, her stomach cramping. Her forehead was clammy and she was sweating. Dink hated to leave her, but he knew that Margaret wouldn't let anything happen to her.

"Hey," Dink said as he sat down on Laci's bed to tell her good-bye.

"Hey," Laci said weakly, trying to be strong for Dink. She smiled. He wanted to cry, but he tried to be strong for her as well.

"I'll be back to check on you later on. Okay?" Dink said, kissing Laci on the forehead. His lips were moist with her perspiration, but he didn't care.

"Promise," Laci asked.

"Now you know you don't even have to ask me that." Dink kissed her again and started to rise from the bed.

"No," Laci said grabbing his hand. "Promise me, Dink. Promise me you'll come back."

Dink swallowed back his tears. He then looked up at the ceiling and squeezed his eyelids shut. He couldn't let Laci see him weak. Then she'd have no reason to be strong.

"Promise," Dink said. "I promise. But you promise to be strong."

"I promise," Laci said, forcing a smile just as she was fighting a severe cramp.

Dink rubbed his hand over Laci's hair. "That's my little Laci." He kissed her once again on the forehead.

Dink left Laci's room and headed for the living room. Margaret and Uncle Sonny were in the kitchen preparing some soup and tea for Laci.

"I'm leaving now, Mrs. Johnson, but I'll be back later," Dink said to her. "Nice meeting you, Mr. Johnson."

Margaret quickly walked over to him with her arms outstretched. "Thank you, Daryl," she said, embracing him. "Make sure you have an appetite when you come back. I'm going to cook Laci's favorite dinner tonight."

"Yes ma'am," Dink said. "I'll let myself out," he said as he left the house.

WHEN DINK EXITED Laci's house, he saw Smurf sitting on the hood of his car. "So whose nice-ass crib is this?" Smurf asked, hopping off the car and walking toward Dink to give him some dap.

"It belongs to my future, Smurf," Dink said, walking past him as he stood at the gate, admiring the outside of Laci's home.

Just as Dink walked past Smurf to head for the car, Laci had managed to get out of bed and go to her window to watch him. When Smurf saw her in the window, a peculiar feeling came over him. He thought he had seen her somewhere before.

"Is that yo' chick?" Smurf asked Dink, pointing up at the window.

Right before Dink got into the car, he looked up and saw Laci standing in the window. She waved at him and smiled. A huge grin covered Dink's face. Laci couldn't believe she could put a smile like that on any man's face with the way she was looking.

She was in the worst state she had ever been in her life. If she was able to put a smile on Dink's face now, she could only imagine how good things were going to be once she got herself together.

Uncle Sonny must have been right, Laci thought to herself. *A man can't appreciate a woman at her best until he's appreciated her at her worst.* It seemed that her and Dink's relationship could only get better.

Smurf had never seen his man so taken by a female. No chick had ever put a smile on his face like that as far as he could recall.

"Yep, that's my girl," Dink said, waving back at Laci. "That's my future."

As Dink got into the car, Smurf suddenly recalled where he had seen Laci before.

"That's the ho on that tape," Smurf said under his breath. "Oh, hell no."

Smurf was in shock. No way his boy knew everything there was to know about this chick. Every nigga in almost every borough had hit that. And if they hadn't hit it, they surely had jacked off to it with as many times as Dame's ass had shown that tape around. Smurf couldn't let his boy go out like that. He had to tell him about the tape.

"You coming or what?" Dink said.

"Yeah, man," Smurf said, getting in the car. "So how long you been kickin' it with the ol' girl?"

"Not long, but long enough," Dink said, smiling. There was that smile again.

"Word?" Smurf said, nodding his head. "You like her?"

Dink bit down on his bottom lip after contemplating his answer. "Yeah, man. I like her a lot."

Seeing his partner wrapped up in this chick, with a smile on his face that could stretch across the tri-states, he did what he knew was right.

"Is that so?" Smurf said, nodding his head.

"Yep, Smurf. That's so."

Smurf extended his hand to shake Dink's. "Then I'm happy for you, man. Best of luck to y'all."

Dink looked down at Smurf's hand and shook it. "Thanks, man."

Smurf cleared his throat. "So what up, boss?" he asked, quickly changing the mood.

"Did that shit get handled?"

"If it didn't, I wouldn't even be here right now, boss," Smurf said. "I even got a lil' somethin' for you." Smurf laid his jacket on the floor and unwrapped it from around the tote. He then held up both hands full of money.

"Damn, how much was he holdin' on him?" Dink asked, taking a stack of money from Smurf's hand, sniffing it, then putting it back in the tote.

"Twelve grand," Smurf said proudly as he began to stuff money into Dink's glove box.

"Take six for you and leave me six," Dink told him. "You still got the pistol you whacked Marco wit'?"

"Yeah," Smurf said, pulling out the Glock. "I'ma toss it tonight. Marco was the third body I caught with this hammer. Three strikes and you're out. Time to let it go."

"Nah, give it to me," Dink said with a wicked grin.

"Fuck you gonna do wit' this hot-ass gun?" Smurf asked.

"Settle a long-overdue score."

"Dink," Smurf began, "I can tell by that look on your face that you're scheming. What the deal, son?"

“Don’t even worry about it,” Dink said, placing the gun in a shopping bag that was under his seat. “I got a special plan for you. Over the next few weeks, we’re gonna start looking for your replacement.”

“You firing me, son?” Smurf asked, sounding a little hurt.

“Never, yo,” Dink assured him. “You’re the only nigga in this game that I can trust. I’m promoting you, dawg. I’m planning an early retirement, and I gotta know that my business is in good hands. I worked hard to get shit to this point, yo. You think you could handle being the boss one day?”

“Muthafuckin’ right,” Smurf said, beating his chest. “I’m ready to do whatever is asked of me for the team.”

“That’s why I fuck with you, Smurf,” Dink said with a sly smile.

CHAPTER 26

The Big Payback

"CRYSTAL?" DINK SAID into the phone.

"Hey, baby. What you doin'?"

"Ain't nothin'," Dink said nonchalantly. "I'm ready for you to put in some work."

"That's what I've been waiting to hear."

"Remember when I told you that I needed you to give my man something?"

"Yeah."

"It's time."

"Okay. So how we gon' do this?" Crystal asked anxiously. "You comin' over here to give it to me or what?"

"Nah," Dink replied. "You come over here to my spot." Crystal didn't respond. "Somethin' wrong with that?"

"No. Not really. Just that Monique's here, and we were on our way to the movies. The show starts at three o'clock."

"So, it's only two," Dink said, his smile getting broader. "It's all right. Bring her along, too—this ain't going to take y'all long."

Dink hung up the phone and waited patiently. It wouldn't be long now. All the pieces of the plan were beginning to come together. Dame was six feet under, and soon everyone else who had wronged Laci would pay as well.

IT TOOK CRYSTAL and Monique only about a half-hour to get to Dink's crib. Crystal couldn't wait to put in some work for her boo in order to get back in good with him. Her hold on him was slipping, and she had to get it tight again. She would have been a fool to let Dink slip away. He had money, power, and respect. What more could a girl want?

When Crystal and Monique showed up at his house, Dink got right down to business.

"Look," he said to Crystal, handing her the bag holding the gun Smurf had given him. "Take this shit to my man, Stoney, up the way. Just hand him the bag and break out. That's all you gotta do. He ain't gon' ask you no questions, so don't ask him none either."

"I got you, boo," Crystal said, winking at Monique. "When I get finished with this, maybe we can spend some time together. It's been a while since I've had any," she added, moving in close to Dink.

"Crystal," he said, kissing her once on each cheek, "you pull this off and you're gonna get more time than you can handle."

"That's a bet. Come on, Mo." Crystal led Monique out Dink's front door. What Dink didn't know was that Crystal had fucked Stoney once or twice. She figured that once she dropped the gun off, she could crack on Stoney for some dick and a little pocket money, then do the same with Dink. Little did she know, the shit was about to hit the fan.

Once Crystal had the tainted burner in hand and was on

her way to meet who she thought was going to be Stoney, Dink wasted no time calling the authorities. He made himself sound as dramatic as possible when he told the police that there was a crazy girl in a red tank top, green Damage jeans, and red Reebok Classics shooting a gun outside. He gave them the address to where she was going and hung up.

Just as Dink was hoping, a police unit was dispatched. A description of the supposed shooter was put out with the added label of "armed and dangerous." Everything had been timed to perfection. By Crystal bringing Monique along, the plan would work out even better than Dink had expected. He couldn't help but laugh when he thought about how he would kill two birds with one Stoney.

As soon as Crystal and Monique reached the Jackson Projects, the police were rolling up. Spotting Crystal's red and green outfit and the bag she held, they knew they had their suspect.

"Police! Hold it right there!" the officer in the passenger's seat yelled.

The two girls didn't think the police were talking to them, so they kept walking.

"I said freeze, goddammit!" the officer repeated. "You, in the red, drop the bag, put your hands up, and back away from it!"

Neither Crystal nor Monique knew what to do. The two were frozen in place.

Monique panicked. "Oh, shit, Crystal! They're fuckin' talking to us. What the fuck we gon' do?"

All they could see was the squad cars' spinning red lights, which mixed with the blaring summer sun made it hard for them to see. All they could hear were the shouts from the police and their own pounding heartbeats. Crystal was petrified. She knew that if the police checked the bag, she was going to jail.

Monique didn't have a record, so she was good. Crystal, on the other hand, had an open case for possessing stolen property. Monique had boosted a leather coat with fox fur trim, but when it didn't fit her, she gave it to Crystal. Crystal's greedy ass tried to take it back to get the money for it and the son of a bitch still had the security sensor buried in the inside seam. The store had received only five pieces of that particular designer style. They could account for the sales of all but one—the one Crystal just happened to have been returning. Crystal caved in and began insisting that she wasn't the one who stole it, but when she wouldn't give the name of the person who gave it to her, they charged her. Dink told Crystal that she would be straight, that they were just fuckin' with her because she wouldn't give up any names. He knew the case would be thrown out, but for added security, he gave Crystal two grand to retain an attorney. Instead of using the money for what she was supposed to, she went shopping and drinking with the girls. Needless to say, the court date had come and gone without Crystal making an appearance.

"Crystal, they gon' shoot us." Monique was starting to hyperventilate.

"Get on the fucking ground," said the cop with his gun drawn. Two other police units had arrived on the scene, all jumping out of their squad cars and drawing their guns.

Monique hit the ground with her arms outstretched, but Crystal's legs wouldn't budge. Crystal was sweating so heavily that the paper bag she carried under her arm had become soaked. It looked as though she was carrying a bag of fried chicken straight from the grease.

"Drop the fucking gun, goddammit!" a cop yelled.

"Wait!" Crystal screamed. "I'll give it to you!"

"Crystal," Monique cried, "just drop the bag. Stop talkin' to them and just drop the bag!"

Crystal had never been so scared in her life. All she wanted to do was give them the gun, go home, and pretend that none of this had ever happened. Fuck Dink. Fuck pleasing him. But then the unthinkable occurred.

The weight of the gun was too much for the bag to hold, sending it crashing to the concrete. The impact made the gun go off, hitting Monique in the leg. Hearing the shot, the police opened fire on Crystal. Her chest and legs exploded with the bullets that struck her body. With each blow, Crystal's life flashed before her eyes. After the first bullet she was in shock. Her thoughts were on Laci; she wondered if the pain she'd caused her hurt this bad.

"Nooo!" Monique screeched. She completely lost it at the sight of her friend lying on the pavement next to her. She jumped up from the ground and looked around, wild-eyed. No one was certain whether it was out of fear or stupidity, but something made Monique take off running. She took three steps before the pain from her wound made her collapse. Sure that she was unarmed, the police tackled and arrested her.

HOURS AFTER THE shootout, the streets told Dink about the death of his girl. Immediately, he was ghost. People thought that he was taking it hard, staying in hiding until the funeral, if there was going to be a funeral. Once Dink hung up the phone with Crystal, he'd made two calls. The first was to Smurf, telling him to meet him at his business apartment on Gun Hill Road. He instructed him to bring all of his necessary belongings with him. Unsure of what his boss was asking him, Smurf dumped some clothes, cassette tapes, and sneakers into two duffle bags and hopped in a cab.

"Hey man, I got here as fast as I could." Smurf was out of breath and confused. Dink locked the door behind him and was silent. "Dink?" Smurf followed him into the living room, where all of Dink's money was on the dining room table. On the floor was a huge Louis Vuitton traveling trunk. "Where we going?" Dink motioned for him to put his bag down.

"We're not going anywhere." Smurf was beyond confused. Dink smiled. "*I'm* going." Smurf let out a deep breath; his heart hurt. "I'm leaving this place. I've done all that I could do for you, Marco, Dame, shit . . . even Crystal. I got to do for me now." Smurf was frozen. In his mind, he was battling whether to cry for the first time since those tears streamed down his fifteen-year-old face that fateful spring day he crossed paths with Dink or wild out and go off on Dink—the only man that ever loved him like a son. "Don't be mad, Smurf. I'm gonna always take care of you."

"How? You fuckin' leaving . . . leaving me here. What am I supposed to do?" Smurf pulled out his gun and pointed it to the ceiling. "This is all I know."

"Naw, my lil' man, you know way more. That's why I'm leaving this all to you. You're the man now."

"What?" Smurf placed the gun on the table. "Leaving what to me?"

"The South Bronx, baby. It's yours. I laid the foundation. You got rid of the suckas."

Smurf cracked a smile. All these years he had been content with his role. He'd never wanted more than what Dink gave him. Now, he was being given an empire.

"Here." Dink threw Smurf a set of keys.

"What's this?"

"A kingpin has to have a castle. I'm giving you this apartment. Don't worry, I own the building. You'll never have to move."

Smurf looked like he had just seen a ghost. "You didn't know a nigga knew how to invest. There's more to life than crime, drugs, and bullshit," Dink joked.

"Damn, Dink. This is a lot for a nigga to process right now." Smurf took a seat at the table. "You leave me this too?" he said, pointing at the mound of $500,000.

"Hell, no!" Dink laughed. "Naw, I left you some money in the safe. Don't worry, before I leave here I'll give you the codes to everything." Dink walked past Smurf and started getting things together.

"Dink?"

"Huh?"

"Where are you going?" Smurf's voice sounded like a child's; the cold-blooded killer was nowhere to be found.

Dink turned around, hearing the sadness in Smurf words. "I'm going to get my shit together."

"SO, MS. DANIELS, could you please state the name of your friend that you were with today?" The detective was sitting in a chair, taking notes, while an armed uniform officer stood by the door. Monique was handcuffed to the hospital bed. She had been out of surgery to remove the bullet from her leg for over two hours and was dazed but coherent.

"Crystal Moore."

"And where did Ms. Moore get the gun from?"

Monique bit her lip; a single tear rolled down her face. "Tonette Thomas. She lives with her boyfriend, a big-time drug dealer named Dame on Morris Ave."

THE SECOND CALL Dink made after learning about Crystal's death was to Laci. She was ecstatic when he told her the good news—

instead of just taking her to the rehab in North Carolina, he was going to be moving down there with her. Later that night he arrived at her door with a trunk full of clothes, a duffle bag full of money, and his prized Benz.

Margaret, Laci, and Dink worked out the finishing touches of their plan. The following day all of them were going to drive down to North Carolina. Since Laci was a minor, her mother was going to have to admit her. Dink was going to look for a two-bedroom apartment—the extra room would be for Margaret when she came to visit. His other task was to enroll in a GED program.

Considering all that Dink was doing for her and Laci, Margaret agreed to do something for him. There was no way Dink could carry around that much money without setting off an alarm. So, Margaret deposited it into Laci's trust fund. When her eighteenth birthday rolled around on August 11, she'd have access to it in addition to the cool million her father had left her.

Dink would never speak again of what happened on that day. He knew that Laci was way too fragile to hear about Crystal.

And from then on, the only person that existed for Laci from her time chillin' in the South Bronx was Dink.

CHAPTER 27

Boston University

Fall 1989

"MARK MY WORDS, without knowledge you're all bound for the welfare line or the penitentiary," said Mr. Giencanna, the instructor for the Introduction to Philosophy class. Nobody was trying to hear him, and he proceeded with the daily roll call.

"Mr. Jason Abbott?" Mr. Giencanna called out, fixing his glasses on his hawklike nose.

"Here," a young man in the rear spoke up.

"Casey Bernard?"

"Right here," said another male's voice.

"Miss Natalie Farmer?"

This time there was no reply.

"Natalie Farmer?" he repeated.

A young man wearing a blue and gray varsity jacket nudged Natalie, who was sitting at her desk, dozing off.

"What?" she said sleepily, and with an attitude.

He nodded toward their instructor. "Roll call. That's what."

"I'm here, Mr. Giencanna, sir," Natalie said, wiping around her mouth.

"Stay with us, please, Miss Farmer," said Mr. Giencanna. Although he phrased it like a request, Natalie knew by his stern tone and the piercing look in his eyes that it was, without a doubt, an order.

Mr. Giencanna cleared his throat and continued. "Miss Julacia Johnson?"

Once again there was no reply. The classroom was silent as everyone looked around to see if there was another nodding student somewhere. Everyone appeared to be wide awake.

"Perhaps we have another sleeping beauty amongst us," Mr. Giencanna said sarcastically. "Is there a Miss Julacia Johnson present?"

Still there was no reply.

"Julacia Johnson?" he repeated, very much irritated this time. The silence remained.

The welfare line or the penitentiary, he thought. No sooner than his eye looked to call the next name, the classroom door came flying open.

"Present," Laci huffed, as she rushed into the classroom with books in hand. The class fell silent to the remarkable presence before them. There Laci stood, just as beautiful as ever. Her shiny Shirley Temple curls, full of body, fell slightly across the left side of her forehead, tickling her eyebrow. Her moody brown eyes sparked with a hunger for knowledge.

"Sorry I'm late," Laci said out of breath as she looked down at her Movado watch, the same one her father had given her for her sixteenth birthday. "But I'm here. I made it!"

"And who are you, sir?" Mr. Giencanna looked past her.

"Ah . . . I'm Din—I mean, Daryl . . . Daryl Highsmith. I'm not on the list, sir; I just got accepted last week."

ACKNOWLEDGMENTS

To my Lord and Savior Jesus Christ.

Vickie Stringer for editorial guidance and support.

Triple Crown Publications.

Kwan Foye, Robert Little, Chloé A. Hillard for allowing my story a chance to be told. There is no way this book could be possible without your support and effort to start my career.

To all the bookstores and distributors and of course, readers.

Thank you!

Lisa Lennox

Printed in the United States
By Bookmasters